THE SEVEN CARDINAL VIRTUES

CONTRIBUTORS

Kathy Acker is the author of *The Childlike Life of the Black Tarantula* (1973), *I Dreamt I was a Nymphomaniac, Imagining!* (1974), *The Adult Life of Toulouse Lautrec* (1975), and *Kathy Goes to Haiti* (1978), all published in the United States by Grove Press; *Don Quixote* (Paladin); and *Blood and Guts in High School*, *Great Expectations*, *My Death My Life by Pier Paolo Pasolini* and *Empire of the Senseless*, published by Picador.

Leslie Dick, who was born in 1954, is an American writer who lives in London. Her first novel, *Without Falling*, was published by Serpent's Tail in 1987, and in the United States by City Lights in 1988. Her short story 'Minitel 3615' is included in the Serpent's Tail compilation *Sex and the City*.

Zoë Fairbairns was born in 1948. Her published novels include *Benefits* (Virago), *Stand We At Last* (Virago), *Here Today* (Methuen, winner of the 1985 Fawcett Book Prize), and *Closing* (Methuen). Her contemporary family saga *Daddy's Girls* will be published by Methuen in 1991. Her short stories have appeared in anthologies including *More Tales I Tell My Mother* (Journeyman), *Despatched from the Frontiers of the Female Mind* (Women's Press), and *The Seven Deadly Sins* (Serpent's Tail), for which she wrote 'Covetousness'.

Alison Fell is a Scottish novelist and poet who lives and works in

London. She is the author of *The Grey Dancer, Every Move You Make* and *The Bad Box,* and the poetry collections *Kisses for Mayakovsky* and *The Crystal Owl.* She edited and contributed to *The Seven Deadly Sins* (Serpent's Tail, 1988) and her latest novel *Mer de Glace* is to be published this year by Methuen.

Grizelda Holderness was born in Harare, Zimbabwe in 1953. She came to Britain in 1972 to go to art school (Bristol then Central School) and stayed on in London for fifteen years. She now lives in Gloucestershire (with New Zealander, cats, chickens and peacocks) — on the way to Africa and/or India . . .

Sara Maitland was born in 1950, and now lives in East London. She has published four novels, the most recent of which is *Three Times Table* (Chatto, 1990), three collections of short stories, and three works of non-fiction. She has also edited a collection of women's writings about the 1960s (Virago, 1988). Much of what she writes reflects her abiding interest in women's religious experience, particularly in the Western Christian tradition.

Agnes Owens was born in Milngavie, Dumbartonshire in 1926. Married twice and has had seven children. Originally a shorthand typist, she has worked in shops, factories and as a cleaner. She was encouraged to write after joining a writing class ten years ago and has published two books, *Gentlemen of the West* and *Little Birds in the Wilderness.* She has also contributed stories to *Lean Tales.* Last year she wrote a play along with Liz Lochhead which toured Scotland for three months. She contributed 'Pride' to *The Seven Deadly Sins,* and is currently working on another book.

Michèle Roberts was born in 1949, and is half-French. She lives and works in London. She has published five novels, the most recent of which is *In the Red Kitchen* (Methuen, 1990). She is co-author of four collections of poetry and three of short stories. her first solo collection of poetry was *The Mirror of the Mother* (Methuen, 1986) and she hopes that her second one, *The Prodigal Daughter*, will find a publisher soon. Her play *The Journeywoman* was premiered at the Mercury Theatre, Colchester, in 1987. She has contributed essays and articles to four anthologies on aspects of writing. She is obsessed with nuns and food.

THE SEVEN CARDINAL VIRTUES

KATHY ACKER
LESLIE DICK
ZOË FAIRBAIRNS
ALISON FELL
SARA MAITLAND
AGNES OWENS
MICHÈLE ROBERTS

with illustrations by
GRIZELDA HOLDERNESS

edited by
ALISON FELL

SERPENT'S
TAIL

The publishers thank Mark Ainley, Martin Chalmers, John Kraniauskas, Bob Lumley, Enrico Palandri, Kate Pullinger, Antonio Sanchez for their advice and assistance.

Photo credits for back cover: Léonie Caldecott (Sara Maitland); Crispin Hughes (Michèle Roberts); Karen Knorr (Leslie Dick); Mark Nash (Alison Fell); John Petherbridge (Zoë Fairbairns); Kate Simon (Kathy Acker).

Library of Congress Catalog Card Number: 90-60281

British Library Cataloguing in Publication Data
The seven cardinal virtues.
    1. Short stories in English, 1945 – Anthologies
    I. Fell, Alison
    823.0108
    ISBN 1-85242-169-X

First published 1990 by
Serpent's Tail, 4 Blackstock Mews, London N4

Typeset in 10/13pt Garamond by AKM Associates (UK) Ltd, London

Printed on acid-free paper by
Nørhaven A/S, Viborg, Denmark

CONTENTS

There was an old woman in China who had supported a monk for over twenty years. She had built a little hut for him and fed him while he was meditating. Finally she wondered just what progress he had made in all this time.

To find out, she obtained the help of a girl rich in desire. 'Go and embrace him,' she told her, 'and then ask him suddenly: "What now?"'

The girl called upon the monk and without much ado caressed him, asking him what he was going to do about it.

'An old tree grows on a cold rock in winter,' replied the monk somewhat poetically. 'Nowhere is there any warmth.'

The girl returned and related what he had said.

'To think I fed that fellow for twenty years,' exclaimed the old woman in anger. 'He showed no consideration for your need, no disposition to explain your condition. He need not have responded to passion, but at least he should have evidenced some compassion.'

She at once went to the hut of the monk and burned it down.

(From the *Shaseki-Shu*, Japan, 13th C.)

INTRODUCTION

As laid down by the Greek philosophers, the four cardinal virtues — Prudence, Temperance, Fortitude and Justice — were a recipe for moderation, measure, and correct conduct. Later Roman and medieval moralists like Ambrose and Aquinas took over the original list and added the three theological virtues of Faith, Hope and Charity (Love), distinguished by St Paul as the specifically Christian virtues.

Compared to the Seven Deadly Sins, which through the ages have never failed to catch the popular imagination, the Seven Virtues lack a certain verve. In their struggle with the forces of the World, the Flesh and the Devil for the souls of men, there's always a feeling that the contest is unequal and that, in religious iconography at least, excess refreshes the parts that moderation doesn't reach. As I mentioned in the introduction to *The Seven Deadly Sins*, all the Deadly Sins except Lechery were conventionally represented as male, whereas the Seven Cardinal Virtues were exclusively female. Even ethics were gendered, then, corralling us in the familiar dichotomy of virgin/whore. Either we leak virtue effortlessly, like milk, or else we're the temptress, unconstrained lust; always we're Otherness, the fabric of male projection. But perhaps in this unequal apportioning of virtue there was a concern that the glue wasn't strong enough to stick. By the 14th century the Franciscan ethic had permeated the social fabric to produce attitudes of renunciation which were seen to be particularly fitting to the female. The specifically feminine virtues enjoined so forcibly by the sermons and secular handbooks of the times were peculiarly lacklustre: patience, modesty, obedience, chastity, humility.

To add to the overkill, virtue transmutes through the ages and becomes singular: with the unerringness of obsession it slips down from nobler parts and takes up residence between our thighs. For Sir Lancelot virtue was a prize to be won by epic deeds; for Guinevere and the rest of us, it was a given, and we could only lose it. Relegated to the territory of the body, then, we defend and prize a property of emptiness, abstinence, lack — and if we aren't assiduous enough, others may well go to war to defend it for us. Like the Daughters of the American Revolution, we carry in our pure womanhood the moral aspirations of the times, and what could be more infuriating than that? Allegorical to the point of exhaustion, we perch on public buildings, one breast classically bared, and cradle scales or doves or — as capitalism expands — torches of liberty or toy railway engines.

Fittingly, it's the feminine virtues which bear the brunt of the attack in the stories. Zoë Fairbairns' 'Fortitude' is the kind of self-made martyr we've all met, the woman who grits her teeth and clings to her collapsing marriage and can't really grumble, while Agnes Owens's 'Patience' tells a witty tale of plotting and passive aggression on a package tour to Provence. Both narrative and literary manifesto, Kathy Acker's 'Humility' dissects what happens when the cynical and self-protective mechanisms of the publishing world try to make a post-modernist eat her collages. Love in the time of the condom is the underlying theme of 'Chastity', when on a dirty weekend in Dieppe the protagonists find themselves in full command of their resistances. And in 'Generosity', Leslie Dick's heroine dabbles with North American Indian rituals of sacrifice and gift and discovers that in love and rivalry the ultimate power may well rest with the one who remains empty-handed.

Which isn't to imply, however, that we can't find a good word to say for any of the virtues. Charity or love retains an unassailable sweetness when Michèle Roberts cuts away the connotations of soup kitchens and good works and reclaims her as female symbol and the source of all poetry. While in Sara Maitland's playfully allegorical story, 'Justice' is black and born from oppression, and in love with the white mission-worker Mercy.

In seven drawings, Grizelda Holderness contributes her own interpretation of the virtues with images that speak for nature against blight. In each of them there is struggle and resurgence: virtue may be a bird of light which freezes two warriors in mid slaughter or a seedling which cracks a corrupt city wide open; always it's the quiet yet relentless antagonist of blinkered destruction.

Morality, like Monotheism, has dealt women few good hands and countless lousy ones, and inevitably the heroines depicted here are far from moderate. Whether starring in war movies, casting love-spells, speaking in Biblical tongues or yearning for the lost babble of mouth on breast, they remind us that today's myths are tomorrow's morals, and that when it comes to revitalising worlds of fantasy and desire, every metaphor we make counts for just as much as every move.

Alison Fell

CHARITY

MICHÈLE ROBERTS

CHARITY

CHARITY

[1]

I have a young erotic mother. Her hair, shiny and black, curves round her face and flops forward into her large dark eyes. She has an olive skin, olive eye-lids, straight black brows. Her mouth is big and wide, her lips plump and rosy as cushions over her large white teeth. Today she's wearing a long dull green mac buttoned down one side and tightly belted around her narrow waist, high-heeled ankle boots, and a red beret, and she's slung her bag diagonally across her front like schoolchildren do.

It's raining. Neither of us has an umbrella, so we walk along arm in arm under the colonnades, up and down, up and down. It's lunchtime. Most people are inside eating. The yellow and grey city seems empty. Except for us. Talking as we pace, exchanging stories as fast as we can. Months since we've seen each other, so many words to turn over in our hands and offer each other like pieces of new bread torn off the still warm loaf. Then she makes up her mind, and invites me home.

We shake ourselves in the hallway like two wet dogs. She pulls me after her into the bedroom to find me some dry clothes. We watch each other undress. Slither of a rose-coloured slip, of seamed black stockings. She turns back the blue quilt on the bed, and I slide in next to her. My mother's flesh is warm. The sheets are cool and smooth. I lay my hands on her hips and pull her close, kiss her soft mouth, her shoulders, stroke her hair, the wet silky place between her legs. The storm drums on the roof. She kisses and caresses me. Her smell grows stronger, like a garden after the rain. She offers me her breast, round and white and fat, ardently we lie in each other's arms, touching kissing sucking biting, then my swollen cunt boils over and I come.

I wake up from this dream disconcerted, still fizzing. I'll tell it to Gabriella tomorrow when we're having breakfast together at my kitchen table, and she'll laugh. She'll be dipping a sweet biscuit into her little cup of black coffee, her feet tucked up under her, comfortable amongst the cushions of the basket chair, her profile alert against the white wall, and then she'll light a cigarette, impatient to tell me *her* dream. Her presence unleashes our words. We're off. Each time we see one another, this jostling at the start, glad galloping down the track of stories. After knowing her for twenty years.

[2]

Auntie's kitchen smelled of the damp washing which we hung on a pulley above the fireplace and on racks in front of it. Our woollen jumpers, the sheets and towels, made a moist tent over our heads. The floor was brown lino, bruised and dull. The sink and draining-board were tin. We had a cupboard for food and crockery, a tea-trolley on which we kept the iron and the radio, and a table at which we ate, read, played cards, filled in the football coupon. It was a crowded place, things everywhere: saucers full of cigarette stubs and ashes, piles of old magazines, piles of clothes ready for ironing, our wellingtons stood against the back door and our two bicycles leaned against the wall nearby. We didn't have a garden shed so we kept the spade and rake in a corner, together with a sack of compost and a pile of wooden seed-trays.

The kitchen was dark, as though it was always winter. We had a standard lamp with a flowered shade that stuck out like a skirt, and a smaller lamp on the table for reading by. Auntie was a great reader, starting with the morning paper and going on to the magazines people gave her, Whitaker's Almanac, a dog-eared gardening book, and crime novels from the library. When it rained we set a bucket to catch the drips. We were quite cosy, jammed up together by the fire, Auntie in her chair with an ashtray balanced on the worn arm, the dog on her feet, and me on the old leather pouffe holding the toasting-fork. Sometimes we had toast with pork dripping for tea, if it was a Monday. The best was sausages, which Auntie taught me to fry over the open fire. There was a perfectly good cooker in the corner, but we both preferred this sort of cooking, like camping. The sausages were beef, tight and shiny they rolled in their spluttering fat. We liked them black and charred, then we clapped them between thick slices of bread and butter. The softness of the white bread, the heat of the sausage melting the butter to gold puddles that dripped down my chin, swallows of warm tea alternating with bites of sausage sandwich, this was a banquet. The dog got the crusts.

The little estate of council houses near the railway line was built to look like cottages grouped around a central green. Low brick houses, with plain front doors with little wooden porches over them, plain windows with white sashes and sills. Built in the twenties I think. Cramped inside, but not ugly to look at, not like the modern blocks and high-rises, and, out the back, gardens that ran gaily into one another, separated only by low withy fences. At the bottom of the gardens was the railway line. Auntie showed me how to leave pennies on the track for the trains to flatten. Sometimes they struck sparks. That was the best route home from primary school, along the little embankment thick with rose bay willow herb and cow parsley. I learned the names in nature study. It was my wild place. I could lie hidden in the long grass, its purple fringes waving above my head, and stare at the sky and listen out for the trains. If it was raining or snowing I came home the short way, by the road, and Auntie would hang my socks and gloves to dry in front of the fire and let me have hot Marmite.

Auntie was not what you would call a goodlooking woman most of the time, except in the afternoons when she got tidied up for her visitors. She was tall, with a jaunty face. She didn't look anything like the other children's mothers, the ones who waited for them outside the playground railings and wore bunchy blouses and full flowered skirts. Auntie wore men's jeans, thick and straight, in heavy indigo, big sweaters. She put her hair up, morning and night, into a turban, and brushed it down in the afternoons when she put on a frock. She always wore bright red lipstick and could talk with a cigarette in her mouth. Sometimes she seemed very old to me, and sometimes more like a boy. She let me play with her curlers, pierced metal cylinders with loops of black elastic, and with her big wrinkled hairpins. One of my treats, when I'd been good, was going into her handbag to see what she'd got, another was helping her wash her hair in the bath, carefully tipping jugs of water over her head until she was done.

That was the same jug Auntie used for me when I had colds, enamel, with stains inside. She put a brown capsule, thick and squashy, in the bottom, then covered it with boiling water. I sat by the fire with a towel over my head and inhaled the steam of the melted capsule, so rich and hot I almost choked. The she made me go to bed early with Vick rubbed on my chest and a mug of hot orange. She made me take cod liver oil and halibut liver oil and gave me boiled sweets afterwards as a reward. My other great reward for being good was being allowed to go by myself to children's cinema on Saturday morning, with threepence extra for a bag of chips on the way home. Being good meant not getting home from school until four o'clock every day in the week, by which time the last of the visitors would have gone and Auntie would be putting the kettle on for tea. Nor was I allowed to disturb Auntie early on weekend mornings. We never had dinner on Saturdays and I liked this. I was free to eat my chips while dawdling along the High Street, and then to play alone all afternoon on the embankment. Auntie would come from the pub, have her sleep, and then we'd have tea together and listen to the radio.

Before she went to the pub Auntie would do the shopping in the market. Tea on Saturday was always a good one. We both loved fried potatoes with onions. Or we'd have a rasher of bacon, or mushrooms on toast, or sausages. I always made the cocoa last thing, she said I made cocoa better than anyone. If it was a weekday I had to polish my shoes ready for the morning, then I'd read comics or a book in bed until she came in to turn the light off. Have you said your prayers she'd ask. And I'd say yes. Then she'd pull the blankets up round my ears, kiss me, and go. Her kiss tasted of cigarettes. If I had a nightmare or if I couldn't go to sleep she let me come and sleep in her bed. It sagged a bit. We slept together in the dip in the middle. Under the thick warmth of her pyjamas she was both bony and soft. I'd wriggle to get into a good position, she'd grunt at me to quiet down, she smelled of face cream. She didn't put her curlers in till the morning, she said they hurt too much to sleep in.

She was a mixture of easy-going and strict. I could fiddle about in her make-up drawer, or the box of old clothes she kept for dressing-up, or her envelope of photos of when she was young, and as long as I didn't break anything through carelessness she didn't mind. When I was small she perched me on the crossbar in front of her on her bike and rode me round and round the little green at the front of the houses. Then she taught me to ride my own bike. She got me some roller-skates from a jumble sale, with small metal wheels and worn leather straps, and waved me off. But she didn't much like me mixing with other children and never let me bring a friend home to tea. I went to other children's houses for tea at first at primary school, then less and less because I couldn't invite them back. We'll keep ourselves to ourselves, she always said. She took me to Mass on Sunday evenings, and we sat at the back. Once when the priest came to visit she slammed the door in his face. The first and only time I forgot not to come home straight from school and walked into the house without knocking and went to find her in her bedroom she yelled at me and threw me out. When she came to find me she slapped me. She was very firm about washing hands after the toilet, please and thank you, things like that. But she didn't mind me getting filthy in the garden digging in the patch she gave me next to the sweet peas, or trying to cut my own hair like I did one time, or repeating the rude words and rhymes I learned in the playground. When she laughed it was a hoarse sound because of all the cigarettes. When she washed my hair for me in the bath she made it stick up stiff in a soapy spike before she rinsed it with the jug. If I didn't cry with the soap in my eyes I got a boiled sweet, then I'd sit on her lap by the fire until my hair was dry and she would talk. About winning on the Premium Bonds or on the pools, or the Grand National. We placed our racing bets through the milkman, but we never won anything.

There was an old clock on the mantelpiece, with a soft regular tick. When it chimed, Auntie always exclaimed: ten o'clock struck at the castle gate! If I disagreed with her about anything she would retort: what girl, you dare to thwart me thus? Me making a noise was a schemozzle, a mess was a pile of tack, me complaining was a performance. Twelve noon was the sun going over the yard arm and meant you could have a drink. A suit on a woman was a costume. She said I kept my eyes in my stomach and that enough was as good as a feast. When she burped she said *pardon*. I loved the way she smoked, moistening her cigarette in the corner of her mouth between her red lips or holding it between her thumb and forefinger. She kept her cigarettes in a little silver metal case, held down by an elastic, like a row of babies in bed, and she had a silvery lighter she showed me how to fill with petrol. Strike a light, darling, she would say, holding up her cigarette, and I would rush to light it for her. She could blow perfect smoke rings, she said she learned how in the army.

It didn't occur to me to question her much about her life before I lived with her. Not until I was forced to become aware, through other children's gibes and rhymes, that she was odd and therefore bad and so I too because I lived with her. She had a brother and sisters, she told me once, all older than her, all emigrated now to Canada and New Zealand. One died of scarlet fever when he was little. A long time ago, well before the war. Then she'd give me a shove: stir a stump. And I'd get off her lap and make the cocoa with the half-pint of milk carefully saved from tea-time. By now the fire would be sunk to a low red mass. Auntie would consider it, frowning as she made her decision, then tip on just a few more coals. To any further questions on my part she'd retort: what you don't know can't hurt you. And that was that.

[3]

Who made you?
God made me.
Why did God make you?
To know, love and serve Him in this life, and to be
happy ever after with Him in the next.

Those are the words printed in the books in front of us on our desks. We know them by heart. It's hard to believe God made us, really, because we can't see Him. Whereas everywhere in the school we've got statues of the Virgin Mary in different outfits. She's far more real. Our nuns belong to the Order of Our Lady of Perpetual Succour. Sister Boniface, known as Ugly Face because of her mole and her moustache, has explained to us many times that perpetual means everlasting, never-failing, while succour is a form of the virtue of charity and means giving and sustaining. The words are written up all over the school in curly script, in here too, over the blackboard behind Ugly Face on a sort of gold banner. Alice, sitting just in front of me, raises her head to look at them, then whispers loudly to Mary, her neighbour: perpetual suck; perfect sucker; and they bend giggly faces over their catechisms.

Ugly Face has been repotting the spider plants she grows on the high tiled windowsills of our classroom. She's forgotten to take off her gardening apron, thick blue cotton tied around her waist with blue strings. The colour of Our Lady's robe, the colour of Nivea Creme tins and the little salt wrappers in packets of crisps. Sitting at her desk like a pulpit she picks earth from under her fingernails while she drones us through our little books. God has no colour because He's an invisible spirit, but everything connected with Our Lady is blue.

Next month, in May, Our Lady's month, we shall be received, those of us holy enough, into the Children of Mary. So far we've been Agnesians, with red ribbon sashes tied diagonally over our gymslips, and gold medals, showing St Agnes and her lamb of purity, slung on red cords around our necks. We wear these to school Mass and to Benediction on Friday afternoons. St Agnes is suitable for us because she died very young. Our Lady didn't die in the normal way. She fell asleep in the arms of St John, then angels came with a silver tray and carried her up to heaven on it. Now she sits side by side with Our Lord on a throne, they look exactly the same age. When you're a Child of Mary you get a blue sash and walk at the front of the May procession, you lead the recitation of the Rosary at lunchtimes during novenas, and you kneel on the special prie-dieux set up in the aisle next to the nuns praying in shifts for round the clock perpetual adoration of the Blessed Sacrament in June, just before the feast of Corpus Christi.

Perpetual blessed suck, Alice whispers. Her mouth nuzzles at the words. Mary goes red in the face and coughs. Miss Barney, the biology mistress, complains girls of our age are awful, always whispering and giggling. She's trying to teach us to be good citizens who'll go on to be teachers and lawyers and doctors and she gets so cross when we go into fits during her lessons when she says words like breast. She was teaching us respiration and she said: you can feel your heart beating, it's just under your left breast. We all laughed, we were so ashamed she should use such words. Also she asked us how many entrances there were into our bodies and none of us knew. She was shocked. But she's a Protestant so she doesn't count.

Mary and Alice and I all chose desks together at the start of this term. Mary's been my best friend up till now, but I'm thinking of asking Alice to be instead. Alice is friends with me but she's friends with the bad girls too, the ones like Karen and Janice who know the name of the sin St Maria Goretti died rather than commit. A boy stabbed her with a knife because she wouldn't do it. I don't know what it was. The bad girls, Karen and Janice and the others, they talk about things like this in corners, then they look at me and laugh. They whip off their hats the minute they're through the school gates and unbutton their macs, they eat sweets on the street and wear nylons at weekends when the nuns can't see them. They talk to boys too, the black-blazered ones from Haberdashers up the road with long grey flannel legs and broken voices and spots.

This term I've been made form captain. That means having to keep everyone quiet before morning and afternoon assembly and in between classes and when we line up for dinner. The bad girls make a row and I have to report them. They hate me and laugh at me, it makes me very unhappy. Anyway, it's lower-class to be bad. Alice doesn't understand that because her parents are foreigners, her grandparents didn't come to England until the start of the First World War. Alice has got hairs under her arms and at the top of her legs. So have I. Once when I was staying the weekend at her house she pulled out one of her hairs in the bathroom and then showed it to me in the bedroom. It was long and black and curly. Mine are pale. I didn't dare show her one. She laughed at me. That Saturday her mother took me to buy a bra, she said I needed a proper one. The little draper's in Golders Green was dark and hot and smelled of scent. The Jewish lady assistant came into the cubicle with a handful of bras and actually touched me. Bend forwards from the waist, dear, she said: bend into it from the waist. She put her hands on my bosoms and pulled them up so they fitted. Very nice dear, she said: very nice.

Ugly Face gets bored listening to us recite the answers from the catechism. I watch her gaze wander over our desks, each one with its sloping wooden lid, inset china inkwell. Like the little houses in packed rows, all the same, down the hill where Mary lives. We're not really all the same of course. Mary's parents are quite poor but definitely not lower-class. They don't have to pay fees for Mary because she's so bright, she won a scholarship after she passed the eleven-plus. On the other hand there are girls here whose parents are rich enough to pay the fees but lower-class. Lots of money but badly educated. That's why they want their daughters to have a good education. You don't have to pass the eleven-plus to get in here, you just have to pass the entrance exam and be able to pay the fees. I got a scholarship too, like Mary.

The bad girls are lower-class of course, but some of the good ones are as well. You can tell by the pictures they paste on the underneath of their desklids: highly-coloured pictures of the Sacred Heart, big soppy birthday cards of pink kittens and puppies. They're the ones who wear scapulars under their blouses, and cords jangling with tin miraculous medals, all identical. I've got a real Italian mantilla, black lace, that Mary's mother gave me when she came back from holiday, and I've got a picture of Our Lady feeding Jesus stuck under my desklid. It's from the Middle Ages so it's not rude. Modern pictures of women with bare bosoms are rude, that's why Mary's father hides his at the bottom of the wardrobe where he thinks no one will find them. But we found them that time when we were playing Sardines. I've also got postcards of women dancing in fields by an Italian artist called Botticelli, okayed by Ugly Face because they're art.

Not all art is OK. Sister Wilfred the librarian has pasted little black strips of paper over the rude bits of naked men in the Greek art books. She lets Alice and me use the library because we don't make a noise. We're doing a project on Charity this term in R.E. and we have to do research. We found a book with pictures of the Virtues, who were women from olden times. Justice had a pair of scales, Faith had a sword. Charity was a lady with no clothes on her top under the black bit of paper, feeding four babies at once. I saw a lady do that once in the dentist's waiting-room. She pulled up her jumper, quick as a flash, and I saw her floppy white chest before she pressed the baby's head to it. The waiting-room was small, with a high ceiling and a gas fire. It was gloomy and dark. It was cold, it smelled of leather and dust and gas. I was sitting there praying the drill wouldn't hurt too much and thinking about what the martyrs had to go through and there was that lady with a bare fat chest. All year long I dread the next visit to the dentist and the terrible pain, it's never out of my mind. The minute it's over I start dreading the next time. The drill grinds away, slow and noisy, and you wait for when it will go on a nerve and make you want to scream. I don't scream. I bear it for the holy souls in Purgatory. The lady's baby screamed and she pulled up her jumper just as though she was in her own home. The Virgin Mary on my desklid isn't like that. She's far more beautiful than the stupid plaster statues all round the school. When I'm crying my eyes out she's the one I pray to. She knows how much I wish I was thin and popular and pretty with long straight hair and not so clever. She understands all this and she still loves me. She knows why I'm praying so hard the bell will ring soon for the end of school. Before Janice and Karen can say anything.

The classroom windows, high up so that we can't see out of them, are open on both sides. Warm air drifts in, the whine of the gardener's lawn-mower, the smell of cut grass, the buzz of bees, the drone of an invisible aeroplane. Next to the spider plants are several jam-jars filled with pink blotting-paper and sprouting broad beans, a pot of cacti, a little statue of St Joseph. On the wall, held up by a wooden bracket and surrounded by glass vases of forget-me-nots Ugly Face puts there twice a week, is a statue of Our Lady of Perpetual Succour. She has long fair hair and outstretched arms and a gold crown. She wears a cloak, and under it she shelters a lot of children. Mary's mother says such statues are in bad taste and won't have them in the house, plaster is lower-class. She's got a little china one of the Mother and Child, white with gold flecks, that she picked up at the church jumble sale for half a crown because the ladies running the white elephant stall didn't know its value. They're the ones who clean the parish church every week. Mary's mother does the flowers. The other ladies don't know how to do them. We only have to clean the church once a month, it's part of our Girl Guides community service. I like digging the old stumps of candle wax out of the iron holders with my penknife, it's really violent. I hate the parish church. It's like a cathedral, but small. The walls are pale blue, and behind the altar there's an enormous painting on the wall with all the saints standing on the steps going up to heaven. It's too bright, it's ugly. Once Mary's mother was giving Father Dean's housekeeper a hand with the spring cleaning and she found the dustbin was full of empty whisky bottles. She brought them home so that the dustmen wouldn't be scandalized. Only the parish ladies know, not the men. They do jobs like weeding the flowerbeds outside the church sometimes. But mostly they are in the Knights of St Columba and run things, like the bazaar and the fete, the parish outing and the pilgrimage.

The sunshine is like polish on the red tiled floor that the postulants have to wash every week. The postulants have to help the lay sisters with all the heavy housework round the school as a test of their vocations, then some of them, once they're through the novitiate, go on to Catholic teacher training college up in London, and the others become lay sisters. Sometimes the postulants get the laundry muddled up and send us back nuns' bras, huge and loose and floppy. I know a lot about nuns' lives partly because of being a boarder and being closer to them than the daygirls are, partly because of reading all the books in the cupboard at the back of the classroom. Lives of the saints. Most of the women saints were nuns. You can't really be a saint if you have a husband. Ugly Face hopes that some of us, once we're in the Children of Mary, will develop religious vocations and join the Order. The best and highest thing a girl can do is become a nun, but if she hasn't been called by God then she'll become a wife and mother. It's not so high, but it's what most girls end up doing when they leave.

Ex-pupils come back as Old Girls to Parents Day and the Christmas bazaar. Alice's mother is the most stylish. She wears chiffon and silk, big hats, and she has red fingernails. She has a curvy figure and good legs and a crocodile handbag. She told Alice she still makes love with Alice's father, at least once a week. When I go to tea there we have bagels and cream cheese, black bread and gherkins. Once we had pickled herring and another time smoked salmon. Alice's house is full of thick white carpets, armchairs covered in gold plush, cabinets that light up full of grey and blue figurines of ladies dancing, big oil paintings, very modern.

Modern art is so easy, a child could do it. I told this to Miss Van Doren one day in art class. She was very cross because Sister Agatha had come in to say we had to learn to do religious painting and Miss Van Doren shouted at her that you could make a picture of a watering-can religious if you felt that way. Then she shouted at me: go on then, do some abstract art and show me how easy it is. I didn't know where to put the lines. I prefer doing my pictures of ladies in costume, Tudor or Victorian. Miss Van Doren said I should draw them nude first and then put the clothes on them but I can't do that. For a long time I couldn't draw hands, the ladies' arms just ended in points. Alice's father laughed at them, mice he called them. Now I can do proper hands, and eyelashes as well. Alice mucks about in art class, flicking paint and so on. I never do, because art is my best subject.

Alice is Jewish but her parents think a convent education can't harm a young girl. All the other schools in the area are either Protestant or secondary moderns. We do elocution and deport-ment as well as all the other subjects, and next year we'll start ballroom dancing with Sister Agatha. For deportment we have to walk round the hall with books on our heads and curtsey to Ugly Face without dropping them. Then she inspects our fingernails and our white gloves. Last summer we had to kneel on the floor and she measured down from the hem of our tennis-dresses to make sure that they were not too short. Two inches above the floor was all right but no more. Alice sits in on religious education and comes to Mass and Benediction, she's in the choir too, but of course she can't become a Child of Mary. Or a nun. The girls who become nuns have a wedding-day after they've been postulants for six months, then they die to the world. It's very beautiful and sad. They glide up the aisle in their white dresses with their hair spread out down their backs, then the habit and veil are fitted over them and they disappear.

But if you get married and have children you disappear as well. Housewives stay at home all day and talk about recipes and babies, they read women's magazines, they go to the hair-dresser's every week and have their hair cut off and have perms. I shall never get married and have children. I might try and go to university, but after that I'm going to become a nun. I shall take a vow of silence and never speak. When the time comes I'll just do it. I wouldn't dream of telling Father Dean. It's bad enough having to go to confession to him and have him call me by my name when he gives me my penance. I'd never tell him what I thought about anything. I tell him the same sins every week, quarrelling with my schoolfriends and talking in the cloakroom, and he always gives me three Hail Marys.

Father Dean doesn't like the nuns much. He calls them the holy hens. He said that last time he came to dinner at Mary's house, one weekend when I was staying. He laughed, and put out his glass for more wine. Mary's mother had made egg and bacon tart but she told Father Dean it was called Quiche Lorraine. She had put a lace cloth and candles on the table and was wearing her best dress and Mary's father was wearing the suit he puts on when he goes to the Knights of St Columba. Mary's mother laughed at everything Father Dean said. I don't think a married woman should behave like that. It's not fair on Mary's father. She says he works so hard that when he comes home every night he falls asleep in front of the fire and never speaks. He doesn't make much money. He says it's the Jews' fault, coming into the country and taking all the good jobs. Once he said that in front of Alice when we were both there for Sunday lunch. Mary's mother went very red and so did Alice. They both started talking at once so Mary's father carried on, about how lucky we are to be English because the English are the best and what a good thing it is there aren't any coloured people in the Knights of St Columba.

Our nuns have schools in Africa, to educate the coloured people and get them to become Christians. We save up our pocket money for the babies to be baptized. Also we pray for the Communists, and all the poor people behind the Iron Curtain. The Communists kill unborn babies. At school there are two Nigerian girls in the sixth form, and several girls from Hong Kong. When their parents come to Speech Day everyone always treats them especially nicely to show them they're just as good as us. Once when I was with Mary and her parents we had to drive through the East End. There were lots of coloured people standing around in the street. The women were all in party frocks in very bright colours, red and pink together. I felt queer looking at them, they were not like anybody's mother that I know. Here you never see women standing in doorways holding babies and chatting. The babies are always in prams in the front garden and the mothers only go out for shopping. Mary's father says all the Jews used to live in the East End, but now the coloured people do. Nowadays the Jews live in the same neighbourhood as Mary's family. Once the coloured people start moving in as well Mary's family will move somewhere else.

Ugly Face closes her catechism with a snap. As well as her blue gardening apron she's still wearing her blue over-sleeves, heavy cotton gathered at wrist and elbow. Arms folded in front of her now, hands clasped, blue eyes burning in her white face under their heavy black brows that almost meet. She looks very young, she's got a really peaceful face. Mary's mother says nuns look so young because of their sheltered lives with no responsibilities. By that she means her own work of running the house and bringing up her children and giving piano and dancing lessons. Ugly Face is sorry for Mary's mother because she has to go out to work and can't dedicate her entire life to her family like other girls' mothers do. Only lower-class mothers work. Mary's mother isn't lower-class of course. Ugly Face said we should be charitable. Some women had to work for the good of their families and we shouldn't judge them. They had to get up extra early in the mornings to clean the grates and light the fires and get the children's breakfast. Mary put her hand up and said that her mother didn't do that, she lay in bed with a cup of tea.

In her own way Ugly Face isn't bad. Like now, in her blue gardening apron, when she leans forward with flashing eyes telling us about charity, which means perfect love. Mary's father says that in some countries, like he saw in the war, they think moustaches on women are attractive. That was how he met Mary's mother, in Italy in the war. She came back to England with him and they got married. He became a Catholic to please her and now he's really keen on it, he's Secretary of the Knights of St Columba and he organizes all the parish trips. Ugly Face's moustache is just a thin line above her upper lip. Mary's father noticed it at the school bazaar when he was helping her pack the bran tub. I watched him talking to her, teasing her until she went red and burst out laughing. He was treating her like he treats all us girls. He's quite handsome, Mary's father, with wavy black hair and a little black moustache. Nuns aren't supposed to be like women but Ugly Face is. Moles, too, Mary's father said, are not unattractive.

Mary's mother was beautiful when she was young, you can see that from the photographs. She says having six children has ruined her figure. Her black hair has a bit of silver in it, at the front, and she wears it in a low bun behind, like a ballerina. She always wears lipstick. She puts it on after lunch, thick and red, and she re-powders her nose, she uses the little mirror of the powder compact from her handbag. I hate women doing that in public, they should do it in secret. But I like seeing the inside of the handbag. And its perfumey smell. Mary's mother can't afford nice clothes though. She makes the children's clothes on her machine and she buys her own clothes from Marks and Spencer. She tries to do things the English way, because Mary's father hates all foreigners except for her, but she's still got a strong Italian accent, especially when she's angry. Foreign food is very oily and greasy but Mary's mother is a really good cook. She says they don't have tinned spaghetti on toast in Italy. She's learned how to cook English food and she's really quite good at it. She can do carrots in white sauce, cauliflower cheese, steak and kidney pudding, scones, lots of things.

That day when they were talking about Ugly Face and whether she was attractive or not I was there for high tea. High tea is lower-class but Mary's father likes it. We were having cold ham and lettuce, beetroot, spring onions, tomatoes and chutney. We have salad cream on our salad and Mary's mother has olive oil, she's not allowed to pour it all over everyone's lettuce, only on her own plate. It was all served in little glass dishes that fit into a round wooden tray. When they bring people back from High Mass for drinks before Sunday lunch Mary's mother fills it with peanuts, cocktail olives, cheese balls and twiglets. Mary and I have to keep offering it round while the grown-ups have gin and tonic and cigarettes. Then we have to lay the table for lunch and wash up afterwards. It's very boring, so I offer it up for the holy souls in Purgatory. I only hope someone will do the same for me when I am dead. Mary's mother said how sorry she was for Ugly Face, denied her natural fulfilment and knowing nothing of real life. That was after Mary's father said that about women with moustaches. In England you buy olive oil at the chemist's, it's used for earache. After tea we had to do the washing-up again. The saints had to put up with things like that. The Little Flower had to work in the laundry with a nun who kept splashing her. She offered it all up. It's called the Little Way. It's one of the hardest roads to holiness. Sometimes I think that after I've left university I might put off being a nun for a bit. Alice and Mary and I want to live in London and be bohemians and meet beatniks. So I might put it off.

When I'm staying at Mary's house I can play with her dolls. The best one is Anya. She's got long blonde hair and blue eyes and she's very slim. Mary's garden is quite big, because they're on a corner, it goes round the house on three sides. At the back there's a little sunken lawn with trellises of fruit trees and long thin beds underneath them filled with marigolds and nasturtiums and forget-me-nots. There's a gap in the low brick wall holding up the trees and flowerbeds, it's Anya's cave. She gets kidnapped by brigands and kept in the cave, they take all her clothes away and just leave her covered with a rug. She's very brave but she can't escape. The brigand chief says to her that she's his favourite slave. He takes the rug off her and looks at her with no clothes on for a long time. He stares at her breasts. Very quietly he tells her that she's got the most beautiful breasts he's ever seen.

Another of my favourite places is under the soft fruit bushes, under the black netting. You can wriggle in to the far end and it's a completely secret place, black earth and grass and weeds and the raspberry bushes meeting overhead. Anya gets lost in the forest. She's in medieval times, she's run away from her parents' castle dressed as a boy, she's following the robbers' army. She's supposed to hate the robber chief but secretly she's in love with him. He finds her in the forest and makes her his page. Then she has to sleep in his tent. One night he discovers she's not a boy after all but a woman. He sees her with no clothes on, with her top all bare. That's one of my favourite stories. I play it over and over again. Nobody else knows about it except Mary, most girls think dolls are for playing mothers and babies. Grown-ups are stupid. They can't remember what it's like to be my age. I've sworn to myself I'll never forget what it's like to be ten, and now eleven. I don't know why.

I don't remember my parents. Auntie told me they died in a plane crash when I was two, coming back from holiday. I was lucky they left me with my aunt or I'd have been dead too. I don't miss them at all because I can't remember them. I'm very lucky because first of all Auntie adopted me, then when I got too much for her the nuns let me be a full time boarder. They want to give me the best possible chance. In olden times orphans had to live in the workhouse and were dependent on charity, the same as the African children are dependent on us nowadays. Charity means people giving their loose change. Catholic orphans had the worst time because the English hated Catholics and didn't want them to get good jobs. The Foundress started the Sisters of Our Lady of Perpetual Succour especially to care for the Catholic girls and their babies, her nuns rescued them and put them into their orphanages. They brought them up to be good Catholics and not to be afraid, they got some of them fostered or adopted in good Catholic homes, and they looked after the rest of them in the orphanages. Some of the orphans had mothers but the mothers knew it was in the children's best interests to leave them with the nuns so that they could find jobs and make a fresh start.

Being illegitimate is the worst thing you can be. Another word for it is bastard. It means you haven't got a father and that your mother isn't married and that she did something really terrible and lower-class. It is very shocking and dirty. It's like an extra dose of original sin and it never rubs off. People whisper and point when they see an illegitimate person. Janice and Karen said I was but it isn't true.

Ugly Face is walking up and down by the blackboard now, her hands wrapped in her blue apron. All the nuns walk like that, with their hands out of sight under their scapulars. I tried it, it's quite comfortable. I've also tried the effect of a nun's veil. I do it with a bath towel. But my face is so plump. I wish I had dark eyes and high cheekbones, then a veil might really suit me. Ugly Face is talking about history now. She's saying we shouldn't celebrate Bonfire Night because it's an anti-Catholic feast, it's about burning Catholics. Guy Fawkes was a Catholic. When you burn the guy you're burning a Catholic.

Mary's father lets them have fireworks though, because he wasn't a Catholic until he grew up and he loves letting off rockets.

He hates the Irish even though so many of them are Catholics. Mary's mother says Irish Catholics are different from Italian Catholics, the Pope is always Italian. Ugly Face says the Irish are best and that we should pray for the Jews and the Protestants and the pagans to be converted to the One True Faith. I'm very lucky I was born here and that I'm English. It must be terrible to be born abroad and be a foreigner. All the foreigners try and come to this country because it's the best. Ugly Face's parents sailed to Liverpool because there were no jobs in Ireland and the people were starving. Some of Mary's mother's relatives came here too, because they were so poor in the south of Italy.

Very soon I should think the bell will ring for the end of afternoon school. I hope it does, so that there's no time for the question and answer session. Janice and Karen have told me what question they're going to ask and I'm praying the bell will go before they've got a chance to say it. I'm praying to Our Lady not to let me down.

The classroom has its own special smell, chalkdust and polish. It's like being on a ship, sailing along high above the garden, we're so high up, on the third floor, with the air blowing through. Sometimes at school I'm very happy, like when we're all sitting quietly reading our set book and no one's torturing me. Last summer, my first year here, we had some of our lessons outside, sitting in a circle on the grass. The big lawn has oak trees on it, with benches. That's the only part we're allowed in, except for the tennis courts below. Further down is a sort of wild part, with very long grass, and a pond, and a little path winding in and out of the trees, and a hut with a statue of Our Lady. I went down there once with Mary and Alice, it was private and hidden, like being under the raspberry bushes, only even better because it was forbidden. We lay in the grass and told secrets.

Far away on one side of the lawn is the nuns' cemetery, with white crosses and rosebushes. Far away on the other side is the convent proper, the part we can never go into. At the back of it are three arches which give onto the nuns' part of the garden, and sometimes you can see the novices walking up and down there with the novice mistress in their white veils. We're not supposed to look at them.

The nuns also have a walled kitchen garden. Once, for a dare, I looked through the door in the wall to see what it was like. There were rows of cabbages and leeks in square plots, with narrow paths between them, and there were fruit trees trained round the walls. There were beehives in one corner, and a compost heap, and sweet peas. It was so peaceful and quiet. One of the lay sisters was digging. She looked up and saw me so I ran away, but she couldn't get me into trouble because she didn't know my name. We're not allowed to talk to the lay sisters.

The thing about the convent that really fascinates me is all the places we're not allowed. I long and long to know what it's like inside the nuns' part. It's there, so close you can touch it, but you can't go in. You can't see what it's like. It's dark, and invisible, you can only imagine it. It's a secret house side by side with the one you know, like in the story when the girl walks through the mirror into the world behind it. The daygirls' houses are ordinary sized and modern, with lots of windows and no dark places or secret places. When I'm staying with Mary and Alice we can go wherever we want in them. We know them inside out. There aren't any surprises. Whereas the convent is over a hundred and fifty years old, the main bit. You come into the round entrance hall, it's all white pillars and a carved white fireplace and pictures on the ceiling. Opposite is the library, done by a decorator called Adam, with another big white fireplace and more pillars. To the left is the Red Passage, dark and low with red tiles on the floor, which leads to the school part, and on the right is a narrow black corridor, more like a tunnel really, which leads through into the cloister. We turn right into the cloister and get into chapel, into the main part. We're not allowed to turn left, because that's the nuns' cloister, it goes into the convent. More than anything I want to be able to walk around that corner and see what's there. But of course I can't. It's completely impossible. It's a forbidden place.

So there's this whole half of the building I'll never be able to see inside. Not unless I become a nun. We're only allowed through the white entrance hall on the way to the chapel. There's a separate entrance for the school, in the big yard, that leads straight into the cloakrooms. I often pay a visit to the Blessed Sacrament at lunchtime so that I can go down the black tunnel and along the cloister.

Ugly Face says the nuns' food is much worse than ours, she says we're lucky to get such food. We find that hard to believe. We get thin grey meat full of gristle and fat, carrot dice tasting of soap, watery cabbage, lettuce with no salad cream. The chips are best, we get those on Fridays with fried fish which is mostly thick batter. When we have blancmange, which is white and wobbly with a glacé cherry on top, the big girls call it an Agatha. They laugh quietly so Sister Agatha won't hear. St Agatha was a martyr who had her bosoms torn off. When it's your turn to be a server you eat after everybody else and you get more food, the kitchen nuns keep it back for you. At table the big girls serve out the food and always give themselves the most. We're not allowed to talk until Sister Agatha rings her little bell, and it's like waiting in the mornings for assembly to begin, it's almost impossible not to talk. Then you have to stand up and own up to talking and everyone looks at you. If you stand up too often you get sent to Sister Superior. She has a terrifying face, white, like a cat's, she has gimlet eyes and a cold quiet voice. Getting sent to see her in her office is the worst thing that can happen to you, apart from being expelled. Two of the boarders got expelled last term, they were found in bed together. I didn't understand why that was so disgusting, Karen and Janice were giggling about it in class, those two girls did something we aren't supposed to know about. I wish I knew what it was. Alice and Mary both knew but they wouldn't tell me.

Another disgusting thing that happened was to Mademoiselle, she went for a walk in the far end of the park that's next to the school, and a man attacked her. He jumped out of the bushes onto her, she pleaded with him not to, then she ran away. Sister Agatha told us about it at morning assembly. She was very upset about what all the parents would think and said we must never go for walks in the park by ourselves, especially not down the far end. We always have to stay in full view of whoever's taking recreation. It always used to be Sister Matthew. She left soon after she was professed, she went off to the Poor Clares, which is a much stricter order. They sleep sitting up on bare boards with all their clothes on and they never speak. They are real con-templatives. Sister Matthew always walked around as though she was in a trance, with a dreamy expression on her face. She wasn't much good at keeping us in order. At first she took us for R.E. But Karen and Janice, and Pearl, one of the girls from Hong Kong, started to torture her by asking her questions she couldn't answer. Pearl's going to be a convert, she pretended she really wanted to know about theology. She said to Sister Matthew: if Mary was the mother of Jesus, and Jesus was the son of God the Father, then Mary must have been married to God the Father. We all giggled a lot. Pearl also asked her what was the sin of Sodom. The next lesson, Sister Superior came in. She said that Sister Matthew was very young and we shouldn't be cruel to her. We all despised Sister Matthew for being so stupid and for telling on us. Then she went off to the Poor Clares to be a contemplative. So now it's Ugly Face who takes us for R.E. and for recreation. She lets some of us walk up and down with her, and she tells us stories about famous Catholic places like Fatima and Lourdes.

I *wish* I could have a vision of Our Lady. But it's never the people who hope for them who have them. If you passionately want a vision you can be sure you'll never have one. They usually happen to peasant children abroad, gathering wood in the countryside, who haven't a clue it's Our Lady they're seeing until she tells them. I would know straight away.

I am praying and praying to Our Lady that the bell will ring. But it's hopeless. Ugly Face is looking at the clock and remembering that because of what Pope John has said in the Second Vatican

Council she has to encourage us to ask lots of questions in R.E. So she stops talking and tells us to make comments. Karen and Janice look at each other, then Karen puts her hand up.

It's about Charity, she says, it says in the book that Charity means loving everybody but loving men is wrong Sister isn't it unless you're married and even then you can only love one well Sister is it true what everyone says that Marie's auntie went with men for money she was a whore everyone knows that it's true isn't it.

[4]

I always liked the long way home from primary school because striding along the top of the railway embankment I could pretend I was a pirate chief sailing over rough seas in search of booty. That day hunger filled me, the wind in my sails. It drove me through the long sharp grasses between low coils of bramble, nettles and dockleaves, the froth of cow parsley. I skimmed along a narrow path worn by others' feet before mine. Our route was the same. It led home.

I was in a hurry because I wanted my tea so badly and because I wanted to ask Auntie to get me some new plimsolls for Sports Day. Mine were a disgrace, apparently, I had been told off for looking so scruffy. It was my last term at primary school, my last Sports Day. I felt I might stand a chance of winning the hundred yards sprint if I had some new shoes to run in.

The kitchen was empty. I threw my satchel on the table. The dog didn't bother barking a welcome, she was too old and fat, and she was dozing by the grate full of cold ashes. I called out for Auntie as I ran upstairs, and again as I went in through her bedroom door.

The room was dim, the curtains drawn against the afternoon sun. Auntie was resting on the bed. Her eyes were open. A burning cigarette balanced on the ashtray next to her. She was wearing her afternoon frock, the one with mauve and blue flowers on it. It was unbuttoned all down the front. She and the man with her lay very still, like in a photograph. Perhaps they were not still, perhaps that is the way I choose to remember it. I looked at her bare white bosom, at the man who curled in her arms and sucked at one of her breasts like a baby.

I fled back to the embankment, to my hideout in the long grass. When I reappeared later, at the proper time for tea, she slapped me, angrier than I'd ever seen her. Her hand caught me on the cheekbone and left a bruise. We had sardines on toast. Quite soon after that she decided that since I'd won a scholarship to the convent school I might as well be a boarder. That was after the two ladies from the council came to see her. She said I would have to understand it was all for the best. She sat on the stairs and cried. I'd never seen her do that before. It was then that I realized that something was broken, and that I'd done it.

[5]

I fell in love as fast as possible at university. I chose one of my teachers, because he was a teacher, because he was older, because he was powerful, because he was kindly, because he was glamorous. He took me to Italy. I thought I'd fallen in love with him but it was Italy that captured my heart. I didn't know the difference.

I bought myself a red satin mini-dress with the last of my grant, and gave myself cheekbones with the aid of blusher. Auntie would have called it rouge. She never met my lover because I didn't invite her to. She came up to Cambridge to visit me once and I was ashamed of letting my friends see her. Her old stained mac and her untipped Woodbines and her out of date slang. I punished her for all this, and more, by keeping aloof, not bothering to write. By then she'd moved to Manchester, anyway, and we met rarely. I preferred it that way.

I left my lover on that first trip abroad together. We went to Rome, so that he could attend a conference on linguistics and

Renaissance poetry. By day he attended seminars and lectures and I went sightseeing. I kept company with saints, virgins, sibyls, hermaphrodites, angels, madonnas. It was the long vacation, Alice had gone to Switzerland with her parents and Mary was in Greece with her boyfriend, I knew no one in Rome. In the evenings we had dinner with my lover's colleagues from the conference. Understanding little of their talk I was mostly silent. I concentrated on the food. At night my lover worked and I read novels.

One day, bored with being a tourist, I accompanied my lover to the Herziana library at the top of the Spanish Steps. Waiting for him to finish work, I flicked through an old book of engravings I picked at random from the shelf. Allegories. The battle of the soul. The Virtues. There she was, Mrs Charity, feeding four babies from her bare white breast and no black square stuck over it. For some reason, that evening I rang Auntie in Manchester from the hotel. I learned that her funeral had been the week before. Lung cancer. She'd never mentioned it.

Next morning, having made my phonecall to Mary's mother's niece in Vicenza, I left my lover a note, got on a train and fled north. In the hot steamy weather of mid-August we stuck to the fake-leather seats. The carriage was packed with young men on military service going home on leave, talking and laughing, sharing bottles of beer. Sweat rolled down my armpits and my forehead, disguised my tears. Outside the scratched window the tightly-strung vines were pale with heat, the hills a blue blur.

Opposite me, wedged in between the soldiers, sat a plump country woman and her plump daughter. The latter wiped away great drops of perspiration from her face, wriggled and sighed. I could see that she felt her clothes were too many and too tight. Finally she leaned aside and whispered in her mother's ear. The mother nodded, and busied her hands at her daughter's back, lifting, searching. The daughter blushed and held her head high. She moved one big shoulder, then the other, then shook herself. Triumphantly the mother slid the daughter's bra from out of the back of her clothes. The daughter laughed in relief and pleasure. The soldiers had noticed nothing. I saw Auntie's impassive face as she lay on the bed holding her man-baby. Behind my copy of *Middlemarch* I was still crying but I was laughing too. The daughter slept, head on her mother's arm.

Once we were beyond Florence and had emerged from the tunnels cut through the mountains, the weather broke. Freak thunderstorms tumbled into each other high above our heads. At Bologna the station was flooded, the underpass blocked. People waded ankle deep across the railway lines to clamber onto their trains. We reached Vicenza in the early evening. Gabriella met me at the station. She seemed quite unsurprised by my phonecall, without fuss invited me to stay until I decided what to do next.

We walked through the warm rainy streets under her umbrella. Once in the centre of the city we went along under the colonnades over gleaming grey paving stones. She took me into the Caffè Garibaldi, bought me black coffee and a brandy, sat next to me at the little round marble-topped table while I finished crying. All around us smartly dressed women lit cigarettes and gossiped. Gabriella's head was close to mine. I looked at her big rosy mouth, her flopping dark hair, her square amber ear-rings, and gulped down my brandy. She began to smile. She nodded at me, waited for me to speak.

Blurting out my story in faulty childish Italian, I discovered that I could make myself understood. I was alone and separate now, no kindly academic lover to translate for me, mediate between me and the world. Talking in Italian felt truer than my usual English speech. Because another woman sat there, delicate and solid, and listened to me with interest and wanted me to go on. Opening my mouth, I tasted ash, I bit into shards of glass, I swallowed dust. The word Auntie meant a warm flannelette back in bed, a tobacco kiss, yet the bed was empty and her mouth gone. I stumbled along, finding Italian words one after the other, rolling them, sour milk, over my tongue: Mrs Charity has had to turn her back, Mrs Charity has had to shut her bedroom door, Mrs

Charity has had to go away. I grabbed one of Gabriella's cigarettes and sucked on it.

We crossed the Piazza dei Signori in the steamy drizzle, arm in arm under the umbrella again, Gabriella talking to me about her childhood in the south. Her small flat, high up in a shabby palazzo just round the corner, had a chipped-marble floor and was walled with books. She showed me the shower, the bed, and left me, propping the door open. A shaft of golden light slid in. Wrapped in a quilt, fenced round with pillows, I dozed in the half-dark, listening to the mutter of her typewriter, the soft gaiety of *Don Giovanni* on the record-player. Soon, she'd told me, she'd come in to wake me. We'd have a glass of wine, think about dinner. Her friend Filippo was coming to take us to a restaurant. Until then, rest. The darkness held me like a pair of warm strong arms.

Our Lady of Perpetual Succour Mrs Charity Auntie my young erotic mother.

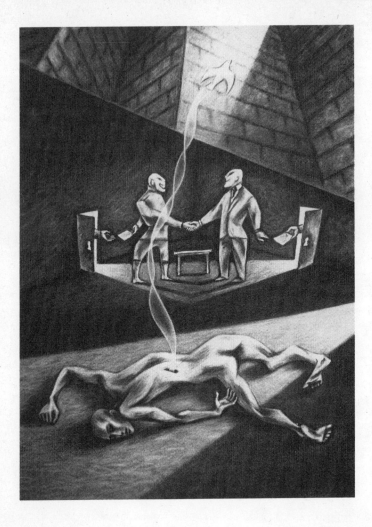

FORTITUDE

ZOË FAIRBAIRNS

FORTITUDE

FORTITUDE

Clive, do you think you could stop harumphing and chuckling over that Giles Cartoon Annual for long enough to have a look at this lovely Christmas present the girls have given us?

Yes, and that's just the card. Julie painted it. It looks to me like the work of a professional artist, not someone of nine.

It's such a good likeness. Anyone would think you'd been there, Julie. You haven't sneaked off and had a look at it, have you? It's hard to believe that you've managed such a good likeness by copying that old photograph in our scrapbook.

Clive, I sometimes despair of you. Yes it *is* supposed to be somewhere in particular. Do you really not recognize it? It's all right, girls. I think he's joking. He'd better be.

Think, Clive. Cast your mind back twenty-two years, three months and seven days. Did anything of significance take place that you recall? Anything of which you might be reminded by this picture, painted for us by our last-born? Any bells ringing yet?

Our honeymoon hotel is the right answer! *Jolly good, Clive!* Round of applause, girls! Give 'im the money, Mabel!

Dear oh dear. It's lucky I don't take offence easily. It's lucky Julie doesn't either. Now look inside the card and see what they've done. Griselda and Martha and Julie have booked for us to go back there for a weekend. In the Honeymoon Suite.

Girls, I hate to think what it's costing. I'm not being vulgar, I just can't get over how generous it is of you. You've only got your pocket money. Well, yes, and Griselda and Martha have what they earn in the holidays, but that's *your* money, you shouldn't be spending it on us.

All right, I won't go on about it.

I'm just trying to say thank you, and you shouldn't have.

I know you wanted to.

I'm not fussing.

I am well aware of the fact that Griselda is seventeen, Martha is fifteen and Julie is a very mature nine. And if you're old enough to send your parents away for a second honeymoon, you're old enough to look after yourselves while they go on it.

I just want to be sure you're going to be all right.

The fridge is full. Next door say you can go over to them if there are any emergencies. And here's some money for the orgy.

Isn't that what teenagers do when their parents go away? Have orgies? What will you be doing, then?

Griselda will be doing her homework. For the whole week-end? Try and watch some television or something.

Oh, you're going to an orgy, are you, Martha? At Dave's place. Seriously, love. Not too late, please.

And Julie?

I don't think that's a good idea, darling. Because Anastasia doesn't want you going round there all the time. Even if she does invite you. Because she's a grown woman, Julie, and you're nine. You should have friends of your own age, and Anastasia should find herself a boyfriend.

If she says that, it's sour grapes. All normal girls want a boyfriend.

She must be nearly thirty. She'll never know what it is to be married and have children of her own if she doesn't stop being so choosy. What do you think, Clive?

You think we should be going or we'll get stuck in the traffic. You could be right. Bye, girls. See you Sunday. Bye.

On our way at last!

It didn't mean anything, Clive.

I had nothing to say so I said, On our way at last! Sorry. Just one of those things. When you yourself have nothing to say, you maintain a manful silence. When I have nothing to say, I twitter meaninglessly. Empty vessels!

Still, if that's the only significant difference to have emerged between us in twenty-two years of marriage, then I think we've done rather well, don't you?

It's hardly changed at all. The gabled roof, and the weather vane and that dear little window. And the dovecote. I wonder if the doves are the direct descendents of the ones who were here we were here before.

All right, you park the car, I'll go and check us in.

Good evening.

I'm Mrs Clive Walton, and my husband and I have a room booked for the weekend. The Honeymoon Suite, actually.

W — A — L — T — O — N.

How odd.

Yes, if you could ring for the manageress, I'm sure she'll sort it out. It may help to find the records if I tell you that we didn't actually make the booking ourselves. Our daughters arranged it for us as a surprise, a second honeymoon. A Christmas present.

Yes, wasn't it? Griselda's seventeen, and going to Cambridge, we hope. Martha's fifteen, and she'll go wherever she takes it into her head to go. Julie's nine. She's artistic.

Here's my husband. Darling there seems to be something of a technical hitch. Not to put too fine a point on it, they haven't got a room for us.

Good evening, are you the manageress? Mrs Forbes? I certainly hope you can. Our name is Walton, W — A — L — T — O — N, we have a room booked. The Honeymoon Suite. Your receptionist seemed to be under the impression that it was already occupied.

No, that can't be right.

No, we didn't cancel.

Mrs Forbes, surely you don't allow any total stranger to ring up and cancel somebody else's booking? Did this person not leave a name?

If you would look it up, my husband and I would be most grateful.

Clive, what on earth is going on? Someone has phoned up and cancelled our booking.

Yes, Mrs Forbes?

The booking was cancelled by a Miss Anastasia Grant who said she was a relative. There had been a bereavement in the family.

Clive, are you listening to this? Do you know of any bereavement?

Mrs Forbes, please don't apologize any more. I am sure you acted in good faith. Miss Anastasia Grant is very convincing. I'm afraid it is a symptom of her illness, to be so convincing.

She is a – what shall I call her?

She is a girl we know.

Yes. I think a drink will be a very good idea.

That's very generous of you, Mrs Forbes. I hope you will have one with us later. If we're still here later. If you haven't got a room for us, we'll have to move on.

If there is another room vacant, then of course we will be happy to take it. The Honeymoon Suite's neither here nor there, is it, Clive? Honeymoons take place in the heart.

I'll have a tomato juice. I wish I did drink. I envy people who can say 'Bring me a double Scotch' and know it's going to make them feel better.

Does it make you feel better?

She's sick in the head.

She ought to be in hospital.

She's always given me the creeps.

Even that first time at the bus-stop. Do you remember? It was pouring with rain and you said, sod it, let's get a taxi. And the next thing we knew, we were in the taxi and that pretty little girl who'd been standing ahead of us in the queue looking so sweet and forlorn with her clothes clinging to her because she hadn't got a mac, was in it with us.

The peculiar thing is, I can't remember how she did it. Did she overhear and ask if she could share?

How would she have known where we were going?

Or did we take pity on her?

Who took pity on her, me or you?

And whichever one of us it was, did she *arrange* for us to take pity?

By standing there in that particular way.

Don't scoff. There are women who can do that.

Naturally we didn't let her pay. That was understood from the start. But was that all she was after? A free ride home? Why's she been in and out our house ever since?

Oh, Mrs Forbes, thank you. Yes, we'll come now. We can manage our own luggage. No, it's fine. It's lovely. I honestly wouldn't have realized it was a single room if you hadn't said. It's a very generous-sized single.

Perhaps the best thing would be if we unpacked first, while there's more space, and then you can bring the second bed in and push it against this one.

Thank you. Yes, please, we'd like a reservation for dinner.

She's sick in the head, Clive.

Why shouldn't I go on about it? Why are you taking it so calmly?

Think of one, then. Come up with your perfectly rational explanation since you're so sure there is one.

A mistake for what? What could any one of us possibly have said to Anastasia that she could have mistaken for asking her to do this?

It was malice. She's on her own and she hates to see a happy family. She *gave her name*. That's what I can't get over. She wanted us to know that she was the one who did it.

I wouldn't be surprised if she fancied you, actually.

And this was her way of expressing her pique that I've got you and she hasn't.

She hasn't has she, Clive?

Got you?

Had you?

Oh. You do know what I mean.

Has it happened in our house?

I see. Our house is just for your courtship rituals. For you to be together. Consummation take place elsewhere. Out of respect for the girls.

Did you already know her, that day at the bus-stop? Or was that the beginning of the beautiful romance?

The beginning.

What happens now?

What happens now, Clive?

Dinner.

Melon, please.

And a cheese salad. Could that be cottage cheese? Do you have any low-calorie cheese? Then Edam will be fine. No French dressing, but if you have a little lemon juice.

Yes, of course I'll excuse you, Clive, but the young lady would like to take your order.

Men!

No bread roll, thank you.

It's sweet of you to say that, but I *do* need to slim.

Could you do me a little favour?

When you cross the doorway on your way back to the kitchen, could you glance into the lobby, just casually? I'm terribly curious to know whether my husband has in fact gone to the Gents, or whether he's making a phone call. You can't tear him away from his work.

He's making a phone call.

Did he look — was it what you'd call a friendly phone call?

He looked angry. He was shouting.
Don't tell him I asked.

Clive, my love. Listen.
   No, don't. Stay asleep. I don't want you to hear this.
   Thank you for that.
   Thank you for making love to me, on this narrow, uncomfortable bed. As you said, leave the Honeymoon Suite to the real honeymooners. We're old hands, we can do it anywhere.
   Thank you for the other thing too.
   I know what that phone call was. You phoned Anastasia and gave her hell.
   You broke off with her, didn't you, Clive? That's why you were so quiet afterwards, and then so tender with me. You've realized where you belong.
   You'll never regret it.
   I'll make it my business to see that you don't.
   I'll lose weight.
   I'll spring clean the house.
   I'll pour oil on troubled waters.
   And I'll never ever mention this.
   It didn't happen.

Yes, thank you, Griselda, Martha, it was wonderful.
   Of course we will, but can we get into the house first?
   Daddy's going to have a lie down. He's worn out.
   Martha, there is no need to be crude.
   I think it was the same Honeymoon Suite. It's hard to remember. Things were a bit sparse then because of the war, but this time there was this huge bed with a canopy and flowers and champagne, compliments of the management. And when I say compliments I mean compliments, they could hardly stop talking about what lovely daughters we had. They said that when you all get married you must be sure and go there for your honeymoons.

You are funny, Martha. When I was your age, I said exactly the same thing, but when Mr Right came along, I snapped him up, and you'll do the same.

Did you get all your homework done, Griselda?

Where's Julie?

How long has she been in her room crying and eating biscuits?

What started her off?

She went round to see Anastasia and found that she'd gone away. Left first thing on Saturday morning. No forwarding address.

We mustn't be sad.

It's the best possible thing.

For Anastasia. She's probably found herself a boyfriend. What do you mean, another one, Martha? Other than whom?

Don't you dare say that, you little cow!

What a fuss, Martha. Grow up, good God, you're fifteen, not five! I did not hit you. It was only a tap. A joke. You made that joke about Daddy and Anastasia, and I pretended to hit you. If you dish it out, you have to learn to take it.

Teasing.

Of course you won't have a black eye.

Griselda, where are you going?

I thought you said you'd finished your homework.

Julie.

It's mummy, can I come in?

Cheer up.

Daddy and I don't want to see long faces, after our lovely weekend.

You don't love her. No you don't. That's nonsense. You had a crush on her. It's perfectly natural in a girl of nine. You liked her. But I'm afraid she didn't like you as much. Otherwise she wouldn't have gone away like that.

Maybe you did do something to upset her. She is rather touchy, and she doesn't understand children.

I'd forget her if I were you.

I'd certainly stop eating those biscuits. You're chubby enough as it is.

I'm going on a diet.

You could come on it with me.

Every time you see me eating something naughty, you can tell me off.

And I'll do the same for you.

Julie, will you stop sneaking up on me like that!

I told you to what?

What I actually said was that as we both had a little bit of weight to lose we could reinforce each other's willpower.

That did not mean hiding round corners while I'm cooking!

I was only tasting it.

And you're hardly one to talk.

You're hardly Twiggy yourself.

You weigh a stone more than a girl of ten should weigh, and I've found sweet wrappers in your room.

Julie, not the biscuit tin!

Eat all you want at meal times and nothing in between, that's my motto.

We'll be having supper in a moment or two, anyway.

I said, in a moment or two.

When Daddy gets home.

At his usual time.

Of course there's a usual time.

I don't know *exactly*.

Why do you have to know *exactly?* You're not hungry. You're a bit obsessive about time, Julie. A bit neurotic.

I'm not laughing at you, but there's something you have to know about life. Grown-up people don't always know *exactly* when they're going to be home.

Last night was exceptional. Eleven o'clock was a bit late to keep you up for your supper, I admit.

But he couldn't help it. Something came up at work.

He isn't always late home, that's your imagination.

And your greediness.

Be a bit patient.

Exercise some self-control.

Go on, then. Spoil your supper.

On your own hips be it.

Anastasia!

Long time no see!

Months and months! What brings you to our door? We're in chaos, I'm afraid; the house is full of eleven-year-olds; it's Julie's birthday party.

Oh, you know.

She invited you.

Clive, look who's here.

Isn't this a nice surprise?

Julie. Could I have a word with you?

How dare you ask that girl here? How dare you?

I am not shouting.

I am not shaking you like a baby in front of all your friends.

Stop crying. I was only joking.

But I'm curious. How did you get in touch with Anastasia? I thought she'd gone away.

You found her new address in Daddy's address book.

And he said the reason he had it was so that you could invite her to your party.

I see.

But I am a bit worried that she won't enjoy herself at your party. She is a bit old for your friends. Look. She's bored already. She's talking to Daddy.

She's your guest and you've got to keep an eye on her. It's your duty as a hostess. Make sure she dances with your friends. Make sure she joins in with all the games. Don't let her wander off with Daddy.

*

Martha, there is something I have to say to you. Something you need to know about life.

It was very generous of you and Griselda and Julie to send us off for that lovely weekend a couple of years ago. We enjoyed it. I never tire of saying how much we enjoyed it.

But if you give someone a present, however generous it is, that is *it*. You give something away and it no longer belongs to you. There can be no conditions. It simply is not very nice of you to keep saying it did no good and we are not grateful.

A present is a present. Gratitude is a bonus.

What do you mean, it did no good, anyway? What was it supposed to be, medicine?

A way of patching up our marriage! A way of stopping us being at each other's throats all the time! Oh, Martha, you are a funny girl!

Griselda thought the same, did she?

And can Griselda not speak for herself?

She's in her room writing an essay?

Oh I see. She's behind with last term's work because she spent the whole time running around after that awful drunken womanizing post-graduate who's just like Daddy and who she'll probably end up marrying if I don't warn her off by admitting what it's like to be the wife of someone like that?

Well, Martha. In the unlikely event of you ever finding a man who wants to marry you, I'm sure Griselda will be only too happy to give you her opinion of him.

Speaking of my own marriage, it is very happy. The occasional little squabble is a sign of happiness. Yes, I expect you do hate it when we yell at each other for hours on end, because that only happens in your imagination. It must be terrible to have an imagination like that. Are you sure you're not on drugs or anything? I pity you.

Block your ears off. Mind your own business. Go and live somewhere else if you don't like it here.

*

Clive, Martha has decided to leave home.

She's not going to do her A-levels.

I said that to her myself. It's madness, Martha, I said, to get half way through your A-level course and then give up.

I don't think she wants to follow Griselda's example and go to university. University looks a bit too much like hard work for our Martha. The way Griselda's never away from her books when she comes home on vacation.

Martha says she'll take any job going. She'll be a live-in mother's help if it gets her out of this — her words — shit-heap.

I said to her, in less than a year you'll have your A-levels, Martha!

Less than a year's more than I can bloody well stand, she replied.

She says there's a bad atmosphere.

I said that to her myself. If there's a bad atmosphere, Martha, I said, have you thought you might be a contributor to it? And have you thought of ways in which you might put it right?

She says she and Griselda and Julie tried that when they sent us for our second honeymoon, and much good it did.

I sometimes think she knows, actually. Well, she always makes herself fairly pointedly absent when Anastasia's around, doesn't she?

Unlike poor old Julie, who saves you the bother of inviting Anastasia by inviting her herself, and then moons around, looking at her cow-eyed, getting in your way.

Have you noticed how Julie never paints anything these days? Just eats.

It's the perfect cover story for you, isn't it, Clive, when your daughter's in love with your mistress.

Very convenient. Except when she keeps insisting on going out with the two of you.

Of course I don't put her up to it.

I wouldn't dream of telling her, or Martha or Griselda.

I might as well cut my own throat.

The longer they can go on thinking of us as a normal, happy family, the longer you'll stay with me.

If they knew what you were up to, you'd lose status in their eyes. And you like status. You like the status of being father to three clever, presentable daughters. If they knew, they might turn against you. And then you'd have no reason to stay with me. You'd have nothing to lose by leaving.

Come to think of it, Martha's against you already. It's probably just as well she's going. She's such a cynical, bitter, interfering girl, she's bound to find out sooner or later. She's bound to make trouble.

But Griselda still worships the ground you walk on. Have you noticed how all her boyfriends are replicas of you? And Julie, well. Julie's the one I feel sorry for.

The way you and Anastasia make use of her.

As an excuse to be together.

As an alibi.

How do I make use of her?

I send her along as a chaperone? To play gooseberry?

Perhaps I do.

But it's in her interests that the family stays together.

She's only eleven. If I told her, she wouldn't understand.

For her sake, I'll keep your secret.

I'll keep you.

Martha, will you let me in please. Open this door.

It is not your room. Four years ago you chose to leave.

Of course we invited you back. Of course you don't need an invitation. You can come back whenever you want. This is your home. But I will not have you locking me out of rooms! And I will not have this disruption of what should be a happy family occasion!

Griselda is very, very upset.

I know you are too. That's why I want to talk to you. I want to get to the bottom of this. The two of you are behaving like children, not a 23-year-old bride-to-be and her 21-year-old chief bridesmaid.

All right, you're not going to be her chief bridesmaid. You're not going to be any kind of bloody bridesmaid and you must have been mad to say you would. Fine. This is what I am trying to sort out. Would you kindly open this door?

Thank you.

Now. Would you tell me what went wrong at the rehearsal?

You realized what?

Oh, Martha, honestly. You're not going to get on your high horse and ruin your sister's wedding over a little thing like that, are you?

It's only a word. It doesn't mean, *obey.*

Why should Griselda and Dick defend it? Why should they get into an argument with you, in the church, with the vicar there? Why should they waste his time? It's very kind of him to let them have the wedding in that lovely church anyway, when they're not regular church-goers and they don't even live in the parish.

Griselda and Dick probably know as well as I do that there's no point in arguing with you, you could argue the hind leg off a donkey. All right, then Griselda is a traitor to her sex. And I am too. Oh, I'm an even worse one. I've been totally subservient to Daddy all these years, and that's what's put the idea into Griselda's head that she's got to be subservient too.

Fine, so you're not coming to the wedding unless Griselda promises to leave *obey* out.

That's your position.

You don't care that Griselda and I went to all that trouble to make your dress.

You don't care what people think.

You want to know what I think.

You want to know whether I think wives should obey their husbands.

I'm not getting into this, Martha.

Because you're very clever and you'll twist my words.

But let me tell you something. Something you might find it useful to know about life.

Sometimes, what you call subservience is a different kind of fighting.

A more effective kind.

I have been fighting for my marriage. And I have won.

No, this is not the Cryptic Crossword.

I have nothing more to add.

Julie, you've been promoted. You're going to be chief bridesmaid.

Because Martha has changed her mind. She's not coming to the wedding.

Yes, it was supposed to be an occasion for the whole family, but Martha's never really wanted to be part of our family. She's always thought of herself as a bit too good for us.

That's a good point. If Martha had deigned to give us more than three days' notice, I suppose Anastasia could have been bridesmaid in her place. She has been like another sister to the three of you, over the years. But she and Jeff will be too busy picking up hints for her own wedding.

Of course your dress still fits, Julie.

It must. We made it on the big side, just in case you slipped up on your diet.

Hold your breath.

Let's ring up that Health Farm and see if they can take you till the wedding.

All right, Griselda, all right Dick, you can relax. Mother-in-law is here, at your service.

I mean it. This is your time and I am here to help.

How are you feeling, Griselda? No signs yet? Well, you tell me what you want. With you I was quite energetic. I wanted to paint your nursery, which of course Daddy hadn't got around to doing. But with Martha, I was quite the opposite. I wanted to lie on my side and close my eyes and wait for it all to go away.

You don't blame me for wanting Martha to go away before she was even born. Honestly, you two.

No, Griselda, I do not want a cup of tea. If I want one, I shall make one myself. I'm here to look after you, not the other way round.

Is that the Pastures New Health Farm?

I'd like to speak to one of your guests. Miss Julie Walton. She's in the Intensive Starvation Wing.

Her mother.

Hello, darling. How's it going?

Wonderful. This time, let's really keep it off.

Here's the news. She's had a girl. Perfect. Griselda's fine too. Sends her love.

I'll give them yours.

You don't happen to know where Daddy is, do you?

I tried, but there was no reply.

No, he didn't say he was going anywhere.

Anyway, if you do speak to him, tell him, won't you?

And drop the hint that a card wouldn't come amiss.

Look at all these cards, Griselda! Your postman will be wanting a bonus.

Daddy has outdone himself. One for me as well? These don't look like cards. They look more like letters.

Why would he write me a letter? I'll be seeing him in a couple of days.

Why has he written you a letter?

Your father never writes letters.

What does it say?

Why are you looking like that, Griselda?

Dick, take the baby from her, she's going to drop her.

Dick, why are you looking like that? What's in your letter?

I don't want to read mine.

I don't want to.

To say I broke down would be to put it rather strongly.

It was a shock, I'll admit.

I didn't know, you see. The wife is always the last to know. As far as I was concerned, Anastasia Grant had always been a friend of the family. Another daughter to me and Clive, a sister to the girls. I never realized she was so intent on luring Clive away.

I don't think it can have been going on all that long. A few months, perhaps. Her engagement broke up, that's probably what started it.

I don't think it'll last.

Seven years. It must be, because my granddaughter is seven now.

Dick — that's my son-in-law — was quite angry with Clive. He said it was a lousy trick, to get me out of the way so that he could do his flit in peace. He and Griselda had enough to do with looking after the baby, without having me weeping and wailing and having to be supported.

He's still cross about that, and so is Griselda, which is unusual for her. They won't have Anastasia in their house.

I see it another way. Clive was actually being considerate. Towards me. He knew I wouldn't want to watch him getting ready to leave. Packing and choosing and dividing things up. To spare me, he did it when I was away. I didn't go away on my own very often, you see.

I didn't do anything on my own.

But I'm getting used to it now.

Martha won't speak to him. She judges people harshly. She ought to be a lawyer, like you. No, not like you, you're a solicitor, aren't you, she should be the other kind. The kind that argues and twists people's words and puts them in the wrong.

Martha could argue the hind leg off a donkey, you should meet her.

Of course you know her, you're a friend of hers, silly me, I forgot. I expect she's told you all kinds of terrible things about her father.

Penniless? Now that is an exaggeration. He's paid me maintenance ever since he left. Every month, on the dot. Usually.

He fixed the amount himself. He told me how much I would need. No, he hasn't increased it. Of course there's been inflation in seven years, dear, but that's hardly his fault.

Julie doesn't cost all that much to feed. She's always slimming. I expect she'll leave home soon anyway. She's twenty-two, so even you can't think he should be supporting her. If she's too lazy to finish her paintings and too self-conscious about her appearance to look for a job, that's her business.

When she does go, I'll get a lodger.

I do a little domestic work through an agency. Serving at people's dinner parties and clearing up. That sort of thing. Nice sorts of people. I enjoy it.

Just a little bit more. If he can afford it. If he's had a rise. You assume he has, in seven years. I don't know. I've tried ringing him, but Anastasia always forces him to put the phone down on me.

You bitch.

I might have guessed a friend of Martha's would say what you've just said.

Keep your help.

Keep it for women like yourself and Martha who don't know what it is to love a man.

Clive. Don't hang up. If you hang up, it'll cost you money.

Ha! I thought that would keep you listening.

How are you, darling?

I'll come to the point.

I'm having a weeny bit of a financial crisis.

It's food. It costs so much, and I don't know where it all goes.

It's because I don't want to be a bloodsucker that I'm ringing you.

Martha forced me to go to this awful solicitor — solicitress? solicitorperson? — who says I ought to divorce you and get a proper settlement. She says there's no reason why I should have to go out charring.

She says I have certain rights.

But I don't want rights, Clive. I want hope.

I know you'll come back to me eventually.

I'm prepared to wait.

I don't want to have to divorce you.

If we were divorced, I'd lose all hope.

If you could just raise my allowance a little bit, and pay it a bit more regularly.

By banker's order?

All right, not banker's order. Too 1984-ish. You prefer to remember your own debts.

Can we meet and talk this over?

Of course I haven't been put up to this by Martha.

Quite the opposite. Martha wants me to take you for everything you've got. And I sometimes think she's poisoned Julie's mind and Griselda's mind sufficiently that they think the same.

Martha judges people so harshly.

But we don't have to do what they say, do we?

They're our children. We're their parents.

Will you meet me, Clive? Will you?

CHASTITY

ALISON FELL

CHASTITY

CHASTITY

Resistance 1.

She'll lie in bed waiting for the klaxon to sound the end of curfew, the blur of her brown hair spread out over the pillow. In the grey light her hands on the dark chenille coverlet are white smudges, plump with youth and still ringless, and if for the moment they lie languidly, savouring idleness, soon enough they will be busy carving butter into whorls, slicing *baguettes*, grinding fresh coffee, for Mireille works in the Hotel Clemenceau and the *Oberleutnants* like their breakfast prompt and early.

Mireille pulls on the black dress made down from her mother's old crêpe de chine, and slips on the short white socks that women wore with high heels in those days because stockings were scarce. She's slender, trim, just past twenty. She'll choose the black suede shoes which are least down-at-heel, throw on her coat, and hurry down a narrow flight of stairs to the street. In the square the Bar des Americas will just be opening, and Pierre Imbert, who'll be clattering chairs down from tables, will jerk his head in a surly greeting which Mireille answers with a curt nod, for there are people in the town who haven't forgiven her for working for the Boches but Mireille has learnt to make her face hard and lie well. A girl has to make a living, she tells them harshly. And now she catches sight of her reflection in the café window: the threadbare coat with the uneven hem, the second-hand dress, the cork-soled shoes which need mending, and she thinks scornfully that if she did what they believe of her, don't they at least have the wits to realize that she would dress better.

In the dining-room of the Hotel Clemenceau Mireille lays out the silverware and napkins and the wicker basket piled high with fresh white bread. Oberleutnant Steuffel, who compares her daily to a Renoir and takes an egg yolk beaten into his chocolate, will prink himself in the ornate hall mirror before beaming his good mornings at her, and Mireille will return his greeting demurely, as she does every morning, swallowing her pride for the sake of France. Sun sparkles on the silverware, on the crystal sugar bowl; the butter in the dish is real and yellow but Mireille's heart is heavy and dull, for the Occupation stretches far behind and far ahead, grey as rats or Oberleutnant Steuffel's uniform.

When breakfast has been cleared and the tables laid for lunch Mireille slips a *pain chocolat* into the pocket of her white apron and carries a tray of different fare — acorn coffee, bread dark with sawdust and chaff — up three flights of stairs to the staff quarters, where the Canadians are. At the end of the bare corridor fat Gunther will be lounging with his gun loose, waiting for his treat like a lapdog. When he has unlocked the doors the Canadians will hold out their mugs for her to fill, and Mireille will place a hunk of bread in each outstretched hand and smile at them, and those who are *Quebecois* will tell her their names and ask her to marry them, all except the prisoner in the end room, the one without a uniform, the one who does not ask her name or beg her laughingly to marry him, the one whose own name, whispered to her in the back room of the Pharmacie, is Philippe Langlois. When the time comes for the Canadians to be taken away to prison camps in the Reich, Marcel has told her, Philippe Langlois will not be among them. Philippe Langlois will stay here in Dieppe until the day the Gestapo come for him and take him down to the vaults of the *Banque* whose thick walls muffle all but the wildest of screams. And that day, the messages from London have instructed, must never come. If escape is possible, Marcel said gravely, well and good. If not, then the only alternative is cyanide.

Mireille shivers now, thinking of what she must do. Glancing quickly around her she takes a note from her apron pocket and conceals it in her hand. When she turns the corner of the landing

Gunther stands up with a lazy smile, his eyes expectant as the seals she saw at the zoo with Maman that last summer before the war. *Pour toi*, she says prettily, presenting the *pain chocolat*, which Gunther accepts with a bow and perhaps even a blush, because he's that kind of good German, kind, greedy and more than a little sentimental. Mireille follows him along the corridor, and now we see that her face is taut with strain, the lipstick suddenly startling as blood against the pallor of her skin. Evidently her mind is fixed on that last door, for she can barely force a smile to her lips as she pours coffee for the other prisoners.

At last Gunther opens the door, and now Philippe Langlois stands up without a word, fair, handsome as Jean Marais, with a proud, angry look. We see how Mireille's hand shakes, pouring the coffee, while Gunther stands in the doorway, munching and watching. When she glances up at Philippe Langlois, his eyes meet hers coldly. *Embraces moi*, she murmurs, and surprise crosses his face like the shadow of a bird before, realizing, he grasps her roughly and pulls her body to his. Mireille cries out and beats small fists against his chest, struggling to break free, and Gunther who is not brave steps forward with his gun cocked half-heartedly, but Mireille stops him. *Mais non*, she protests, thanking the holy Virgin for sending her this harmless sexless man who can be bribed with sweets like a child, It's for me to do, it's my pleasure. Then she'll step forward sharply and slap Langlois across the face. *Cochon*, she'll spit, triumphant in the knowledge that the note is safe in his hand.

Whore, shouts Langlois as the key turns in the lock, and Mireille sees that he has understood well, but all the same the blood rushes to her face as she touches her lips, remembering. For that one brief frightening second she had felt his mouth on hers, and his mouth was sweet, and her orders are to arrange his escape or kill him, not to fall in love with him.

That night in the back room of the Pharmacie Marcel hands her clothes, papers. You are man and wife, he tells her, travelling to the south to visit relatives. Your husband is recovering from tuberculosis. You must take Langlois to Eleni in Cahors. And then, *ma petite* — Marcel stabs a finger at her — you must vanish. No more Mireille Bastide, you understand. I want to hear nothing more of her. And Mireille is sad, sad, as Marcel embraces her, Marcel whom she counts on, Marcel who has been like a father to her, like the father she never knew. Mireille Bastide must no longer exist, he says, and she bows her head miserably, knowing her duty.

Just before dawn a German patrol car rumbles past Mireille's lodgings, and a flash of light illuminates the room for a second. She'll be standing at the dressing-table mirror, her fingers lightly touching her mouth. Then in the darkness she'll move to the window and look out across the *quai*, at the small fishing boats bobbing in the moonlight, at the canvas awnings of the empty fish market, at the town which is her home, the home she'll never see again.

Next morning when the winter sun rises over the *Vieux Port* Mireille conceals the gun and the blue workman's clothes in her basket and hurries to the back entrance of the hotel. Taking a key surreptitiously from the hook by the kitchen door she unlocks the wine-cellar where, beyond the ranked wine-barrels, there'll be another door which leads out into a cobbled yard below the castle wall. The bicycles Marcel promised are already waiting there, so she hides the basket and hurries back, eyes bright with fear, to the kitchen and her duties.

This morning, however, O.Steuffel does not smile or compliment her but sits stern and upright opposite a close-shaven man in the hated black uniform of the Gestapo, a man whose perfectly cadenced French chills Mireille's blood. So soon, she thinks with a sinking heart as her head inclines obediently and her hands place the *confiture d'abricots* beside his plate. There is not a minute to lose.

. In the kitchen she steals *marrons glacés* for Gunther and climbs the stairs with her laden tray. If Philippe Langlois has not understood the plan, or if he hesitates, then they are lost. She pauses on the corner of the landing, her fingertips touching the small crucifix at her throat, the crucifix her mother thrust into her hands the day the Germans came to take her to Drancy. For failure is unthinkable. Philippe must understand and Philippe must not hesitate and all must go well.

When Gunther unlocks the door Mireille smiles *Merci* and then everything moves fast. The tray drops to the floor with a clatter, her hands fly up to her face. *Mon Dieu, il est mort, mort!* On the trestle in the corner, there's a heap of blankets, inert. Gunther lumbers towards the bed, his big round face creased with alarm. And then we see how Philippe is upon him, silent as a cat, pouncing from behind the door. Gunther goes down without a word, flat on the floor, felled by a single expert blow. Sugar crumbs still cling to the corners of his mouth.

Vite, hisses Mireille, locking the door on Gunther's fallen bulk, and they race along the corridor, helter-skelter down the back stairs, bent double to creep past the glass-panelled kitchen door, until they reach the wine cellar where Mireille thrusts the workman's clothes at Philippe Langlois and in the dim light glimpses his white skin, the dark bruises on his thin ribs.

In the wire baskets of the bicycles are leeks, potatoes, knobbly artichokes smelling of fresh earth. And now we ride slowly, Mireille whispers. As if to market. Wrapping her head in a woollen scarf she sets off up the cobbled hill which leads past the castle wall to the cliff road. Without speaking they cycle the three kilometres to Pourville, leisurely as peasants when transports pass, fast and breathless when the road is clear, for the alarm may be raised at any moment and every kilometre is precious.

As the fugitives enter the deep forest of Arques we cut to the Hotel Clemenceau where the officer in the black uniform is finishing his lunch of *moules* and *gigot*, dabbing his mouth with his napkin, climbing the staircase with O.Steuffel. And then, mayhem: the smile wiped from the Gestapo man's face, the Gestapo man revealed in his true vicious colours. O.Steuffel's face turns crimson with humiliation from his tongue-lashing, as alarms jangle and klaxons hoot and soldiers run from the guardroom with their braces dangling, buttoning up their shirts. Snow begins to fall, soldiers rub their numb hands in the backs of canvas-covered lorries, and there's a rumble of engines, tyres splashing through mud puddles, the Gestapo man slapping a black leather glove on the dashboard of the open Mercedes, O.Steuffel's ramrod salute, the car screeching out of the square.

Covering their abandoned bicycles with bracken, Mireille and Philippe set out on foot through the forest, skirting the snow patches. Mercifully the dusk falls early and they move through the moonless night stealthily, eyes straining to make out the dark trunks of trees, hands and legs torn by unseen brambles; only when dawn comes do they sink down at last, exhausted and hungry, in the straw of a cattle shed. We see a gleam of sadness on Philippe's face as he looks at Mireille lying there shivering and separate, waiting for sleep. The gun lies beside him on a pillow of straw. If they are captured he will know what to do, but for the moment he wants to talk, to tell her so many things, this girl who has risked everything to rescue him. Numb with cold, Mireille listens to his voice, this odd harsh French from across the ocean which murmurs on, stops, continues, tells a life story in fits and starts. In Quebec there are sweet-scented pine forests thicker than this, and wide rivers where salmon glimmer; there are beehives and black bears and timberwolves to trap. And although Mireille will think of Marcel's counsel — know nothing and you can betray no one — she'll have no heart for silencing him, for interrupting the flow of those words which have been locked so long inside him. She stretches her aching limbs, her white socks shine coldly in the dim light. So tender and prim, he says. Like a schoolgirl. And she'll see that his eyes on her are hollow with longing. I thought, in the beginning, that you were older. But now . . . taking the workman's cap from his head he'll set it on hers and smile sadly . . . you look so young, like an orphan. But then Mireille feels his hand against her cheek and she's frightened, she's never been with a man, despite what the townspeople think of her. You're shivering, he whispers, and then his arms go round her and she cries No!, twisting away, for it's bad enough that the whole of Dieppe should treat her like a whore, but that Philippe should also think her easy . . . But now Philippe draws back, a dark flush staining his face. Sleep, he says roughly, we must sleep. Unless you prefer to freeze to death. And Mireille hangs her head, realizing, and the harshness of his tone is the punishment she knows she deserves for having misjudged him, and she settles her body obediently against his and feels warmth steal through her like a memory of her mother's arms. In the bed of straw Philippe's heartbeat consoles her, his breath murmurs softly to her. At last she sleeps and dreams of a wedding and a father who takes her by the arm, but there at the altar of the church she looks down at his hand and in the candle's glimmer sees instead the great paw of a black bear, and she wakes on a cry which Philippe's hand stifles. *Ma petite*, he whispers, and his eyes are dark above her. My little one. So brave with Germans, yet so frightened of her dreams. Then his mouth will move lightly on hers, silencing all protest, and her body encircled by his flares into speech, embracing the small pain and the blood which makes her his and the long voyage and the country far across the sea.

When Mireille wakes sweetly in the darkness of the February afternoon Philippe's eyes are alert and his hand stills her, for outside there's a noise of cattle bells. Outside a peasant talks to himself and his animals. He will fetch straw for them, he will spread it out on the snow, they will have warm bellies full as the moon, their breath will steam out in the moonlight. Philippe's hand closes over the gun as the door creaks open. A bale of straw thuds into the shed, then another, and finally the stooped shadow of an old man hobbles in and begins to fork up loose straw a mere yard away in the darkness. His voice goes on low and singsong as before, but now it tells a different story. The Germans are spread out across the snow, the Germans have reached the crossing in the forest, he will put them under the straw in his cart, they will be silent as mice in his cellar, they will have warm bellies . . . Suddenly he peers sharply into the darkness. Put away your gun, *mon frère*. Old eyes see better in the dark.

At Mireille's side Philippe whispers: How can we trust you?

Trust? says the old man. Who trusts anyone in those times? Come. Lucky for you and your wife that the Boches pay no attention to an old idiot.

Mireille pulls at Philippe's arm. We have no choice, she urges. Outside the old man leads them to his cart and piles straw over them. As the wheels trundle over the rutted road they hear the old man's voice sing out above them. He will eat a good stew of rabbit and wine, he will have a warm belly under the moon, he will make love like a bull in the alley behind the Café de la Gare . . . But now there's a faint rumble of lorries, dots of headlights coming closer, shining on the surface of the straw. Philippe covers Mireille's body with his as curt voices break into the old man's babble. And now Mireille chills with fear, for another voice cuts across the guttural German, a voice which enquires in perfectly cadenced French about a man and a young woman.

Woman? the old man cackles back, releasing a stream of obscenities which makes the blood rush to Mireille's cheeks, What need has he of a woman when he has six pretty heifers to fuck?

Drive on, orders the Gestapo man disgustedly, for the peasant is not only a half-wit but filthy-minded like all the lower races. Mireille hears the roar of the Mercedes, and the lorries, slower, following. Philippe's arms are tight and protective around her and as his breath sighs along her cheek she thinks of what the old man said in the cattle shed, *votre femme*, you and your wife, and lying there in the straw she imagines a soft bed and a long bolster, a bed wide as the sea, a bed safe in his arms, a bed which lasts for ever.

Later on a pallet of grain sacks she loves him, her husband whom she trusts, and Mireille Bastide disappears, as she knew she must, and the woman who takes her place will never leave his side, for when she touches his face in the dark Cahors doesn't exist, and parting doesn't exist, nothing exists but the long road to Spain, and the lights on the great bay of Lisbon, and the tall pine trees of distant Quebec. Take me with you, she murmurs, and night after night on the road to Cahors his encircling arms answer her, in ditches and haybarns and packed muttering trains whose first class carriages say Reserved for *Wehrmacht*, and although the mouth which once confided his innermost secrets is now more circumspect, we can see that Mireille will go on trusting with the blind trust of a young girl who knows little of men and has given herself entirely.

At the station in Cahors the *gardes mobiles* shine torches on their papers, their faces. There's a terrible frozen pause, doubts. Will they be detected? But no, the guard is waving them through the barrier, they're slipping through the back streets to the Café Grecque where Eleni will give them coffee and glasses of a pink liqueur which tastes of petrol and roses and tell them which path to follow to the high Causses, where the maquisards wait ready to take them to Spain and freedom.

It's dawn when they reach the rocky hill where the ruined farmhouse nestles. Goatbells tinkle somewhere in the distance but the farmyard is bleak and deserted. Philippe Langlois stands silently for a moment, staring south to where the sky is clear and the peaks of the Pyrenees are faint on the far horizon. Fingering the crucifix at her throat, Mireille smiles at her love: Soon all will be over, she whispers, soon we will be safe.

And now there's a sharp whistle and the men emerge from barns and outhouses to surround them, weathered men with cautious eyes and guns at the ready. But as the men motion them to follow, Langlois rests his hand on Mireille's shoulder. *Attends*, he orders. And now he strides towards the man in the leather jacket, the commander; he's taking him aside. Mireille watches the two men, unsuspecting. What can they be saying? The commander is shrugging, Philippe is coming back towards her, grave-faced. A chill descends on her heart as he puts both hands on her shoulders and looks down at her sternly, so sternly: has she done something wrong? Philippe is speaking. Be brave, *ma petite*. The escape route is for one only. The orders are that I must go alone. *Mais non*, Mireille cries, *C'est pas vrai!* Tears fill her eyes as she thinks of Lisbon, the lights on the water. But now her mind is racing. All is not lost. She has friends, contacts: Eleni will help her. But I will follow, she pleads, I will find a way. Philippe shakes his head. No, *ma petite*, he says gently. It's a beautiful dream, no more. Fury stings Mireille now, the fury that comes with the pain of rejection. Why does Philippe look away? What is he hiding from her? She clutches his arm, suspicious, but he thrusts her back, angry because he knows that he must hurt her. I have a wife in Quebec, he mutters. Now are you satisfied?

Mireille's face will be dead white now against the dark frame of the woollen scarf. Her hands will fly to her throat and hover there helplessly, and Philippe Langlois, unable to bear the guilt that this frantic refugee face kindles in him, will defend himself clumsily with brutal words. Oh, but Mireille was willing, he'll sneer, Mireille was easy. His wife is chaste, she gives her body to him only and only in wedlock, whereas who's to say how many men Mireille has given herself to?

Shock flings Mireille to the hard ground. The *maquisards* avert their eyes and hunch resentfully over their rifles, anyone can see they don't like it. The *petite fille* looks so young, so naive; on the other hand what's necessary must be done and it's no business of theirs to judge the morals of a comrade on the run.

But now the commander signals. They must hurry. You are ready? he asks Langlois brusquely. Bending to Mireille, Langlois attempts to help her up, but Mireille shrinks from him like a wounded animal. Betrayer! she cries, out of her mind with grief, betrayer! and the words echo back from the rocks as with a last brokenhearted look at Langlois she stumbles to her feet and runs away from the deserted farmyard, up on to the Causses where the freezing wind fans the tears out across her face, while in the *Préfecture* of Cahors a message comes, tap tap on the telegraph and curt orders snap out and cars screech out of the cobbled square, and up on the Causses we see Mireille running, running till she's exhausted and can only drag herself weakly through the juniper scrub, she's crawling, she's at the end of her strength, she's dragging herself into a shepherd's hut, a shepherd's hut shaped like a beehive, a hut with a bed of straw, a bed wide as the sea where the Boches will never find her.

He said — on the way home I'm going to lash you to the bowsprit or whatever they call the thing that pokes out at the front. She said she didn't have long streaming hair and her tits weren't big enough but he said oh yes they are or at least they'll do.

Where they were headed:

Rolande's studio had red tiled floors, two rooms with a glass partition dividing them. At the front an arched window looked out on to a narrow cobbled street; directly opposite were the windows — lit all night — of the staff quarters of the Hotel Clemenceau. In the back room, which was the kitchen, the window overlooked a yard devoid of grass or shrubs, and this window had a lace curtain draped over it — not net, since this was no boarding house, this wasn't one of Torquay's savage bungalows — but lace, French lace with a winsome pattern of ferns and a six inch fringe at the bottom. There was a round table covered with a checked oilcloth, folding kitchen chairs, and a cooker with puzzling controls which heated different parts of the oven to different temperatures for different dishes: *soufflés, tartes, rôtis, daubes, petits pigeons.* There was no other furniture — except in the bedroom, of course, which contained a new large pine bed with a good solid mattress.

In the black storm Dora lay flat. Tinfoil ashtrays skittered across the tables as the lounge bar tilted and plunged. The doors to the deck were lashed shut, and the air was stuffy with smoke. The low ceiling of the bar was a patchwork of plastic squares on which designs of gold and black semicircles verged constantly on the yin-yang symbol but always drew back at the brink. Dora shut her eyes. 'I'm sure it's worst at the front,' she said, but by this time she couldn't move an inch — stabs in the stomach, bile, her inner gyroscopes all messed up.

Colin was sitting up with the *Guardian*, concentrating. If he focused on the words the motion of the boat would cease to exist, the imposed structure was his salvation. But this was a strategy Dora didn't find out about till later; on the way over she simply thought he must be a good sailor, not a pallid cheek or word of complaint, phenomenal. Colin's hands held the Reviews section high up and stretched, the top corners pinched between fingers and flattened thumb, like a length of dress material. Balls of his thumbs savouring the feel of the paper, sensual, precise. The second finger of his right hand wouldn't bend: he fell off a perimeter fence at nine years old, caught it, tore it nearly off. He'd told Dora that it was all connected in his mind with his mother, castration anxieties: this threatened finger, this finger without flexibility, this finger which could never learn to play the guitar. He'd bent the other ones to show her, and she'd seen him do Tai Chi soft and circling, but it was true, this particular one stayed straight as a splint. On the index finger of the right hand and the ring finger of the left, perforated Band Aids covered scars where the warts had been burnt off. Dora's last smear showed Human Papilloma Virus and yes there could be a connection but with sixteen different wart viruses in circulation their doctors were at sea. Colin's penis had been scraped, too (barnacles?) but it was the anal exam which had shocked him. Welcome to the female experience, she'd said in the middle of sympathizing: her terrible mouth.

Colin leaned over Dora, glasses slipping down the bridge of his nose. 'On the way home I'm going to lash you to the bowsprit,' he grinned. Want want want, he thought, looking down at her: just because you're divorced doesn't mean you're fancy free, can't she see his hands are tied? Flat out, though, she was comical and it was ironic and he was touched; he could almost forget the dramas about the weekend, the angry badgering Dora, the Dora who wouldn't be satisfied until he said yes.

He sat up straight and dug his knuckles into his backache, the old ache, the ache which wouldn't go. Ought ought ought, it said. 'So you're telling me you're allergic to fun,' his therapist had observed. Sharp, she was sharp. Okay so he had a problem with holidays but look at his track record. All that time and space and relationships went straight into self-destruct, if you couldn't count on anything else in life you could certainly count on that. Well, this weekend there wouldn't be any quarrels, thanks to the plan he'd formulated. On Saturday he'd be right, and on Sunday it would be Dora's turn. That way he could only be in the wrong 50 per cent of the time, which made 100 per cent improvement according to his reckoning. It was the only time he'd ever seen his therapist laugh out loud. Thinking about it, he felt wickedly, supremely clever. He inclined his arm at a forty-five degree angle, the angle of an erect penis. 'You know. Hands tied behind your back, tits thrusting, hair streaming.'

Hands tied behind her back, Dora is erect. A big penis, barnacle-encrusted, cleaving the waves. When she was a girl she'd had a fantasy which soothed her to sleep: a finger-doll who got tied up, punished regularly, tried, sentenced, walked the plank, was resurrected the next night, and so on. Or so she told her therapist as she lay on the couch with her hands scrunched up like tissues, out of the way of punishment.

Dora was accustomed to taking the blame. Her mind buzzed with the questions women ask themselves. Like. Is this a relationship. Will it be. Am I responsible for my wart virus. Who is my body trying to sabotage. Sometimes when she got depressed it occurred to her that maybe she should wait to fall in love before she slept with someone: the old-fashioned approach. Nowadays you were supposed to feel sex first, love later, so that sex became the testing ground for love, rather than the reverse. But somehow this left Dora feeling at a disadvantage. As if she, rather than Colin, was the one who was on trial.

Psychotherapy 1.

'But you see he keeps me out of his life, when his children stay I never see him, I never see Kate and Lilian, I feel he's hiding me, hiding, he just won't read my work he reads the paper in bed when we already have so little time, honestly how long has it taken to get him to go away for the weekend, one night mid-week was a big enough concession, a real upheaval, he wants me to leave him to do his work even on Sundays, says I'm insecure and it's not fair to lay it all on him because I'm on my own and he's got his daughters, responsibilities, compartments I call it, a small box for me in which I flail, small trap baited by sex-love oh you know the picture, chew your foot off to escape and you're only back to lonely, so probably I do need too much attention, too much of everything, I'm always thinking I should be more self-contained and like him needing nothing but how much starving can you take. He wants me to be quiet, be seen and not heard so okay I'll be quiet, shut up Dora, try to take what he gives, passive, slightly masochistic even, could be a turn on, oh I'll be very very good and perfectly ordinary then maybe I'll get it right, maybe it'll be easier away without phone or interruptions to hide in so we'll have to see it through like being married and probably I need to be, oh shut up Dora yes I know but how else do we get our mothers, okay call it containment, nurture, whatever, but men have women to contain them don't they, secure, surround them tight, if he'd only talk about the future, trips and things and dreaming tenderly, is it so wrong just to long for some time stretching and safety to feel important instead of this vulnerable kept at bay feeling where you walk on eggs needing approval he won't give and then I get in a rage he can't take and it backfires, I turn it in on me when really I want to lodge it somewhere not in me but then I can't and it's homeless, my very own orphan so who'll contain it not banish it, shove it off downstream like Moses in the basket or something, this baby, this needy demon that's maybe sort of inspired and arrogant too now I come to think of it but is it so wrong to want to be loved for all the colours you own although maybe you've got to love it first since he won't but it turns into a rage at the way he's so silent, his face so hurt and guilty making me feel awful and then I have to hide it, float it down the river, my secret messy baby noisy excitable keep it for me alone and not be seen or heard, you know, just be good so quiet so very very good but what if I have to upheave which'll make me feel bad accusing demanding because of my starving stuff and not wanting to risk leaving and terrible things when I could follow him entirely except that he keeps me out of his life, when his children stay I never see him, he hides me, he hides his time his space his loving words he just won't let me be important he always keeps me out.

'We must be going along the coast,' Dora said, looking. Yes. Little pips of light strung out. Relaxing now, for the seesawing had eased, and the boat was spanking quite confidently through the water.

Colin jerked his head at the ceiling. He was going up, he was going on deck to take a look. 'Kate was determined to come,' he confided suddenly; his smile was awkward and private and shining. 'Just the word ferry was enough.'

'Right,' said Dora, watching him go. The floor of the bar was cambered and he crossed it on careful feet but his face was dreaming and yes she was jealous but what of it. Her hands flew about her, pushing combs back into her hair; a wetted finger stroked under her eyes to check for make-up smudges. When Colin came back she was beginning to be hungry. 'Moules,' she said, 'Coquilles St Jacques.'

'From the Channel?' Colin looked at her incredulously, his long fingers shuttling along the stubble on his upper lip. His lower lip, now sarcastic, was puffy, almost sulky — a seedy Jean-Louis Trintignant look which always, he insisted, got him stopped at Customs. 'Well if you want to glow in the dark.'

'Come on,' said Dora. 'It can't be that bad.' Our bad season, she thought. Oh yes it can. February the oyster month; his grey city coat, the bag of folders and essays to prove how very difficult it was for him to get away. I want to love him but he snaps shut like a briefcase. Oh I know. He's trying. I paint my fingernails red as Chinese lanterns, long almond shapes; I dig my nails into his cock, we like to do this.

Colin frowned at her. He did in fact look catastrophically tired. 'Most polluted waterway in the world for Christ's sake.' He gave her the mussel lecture — how they're allergic to some special paint used to protect the hulls of ships from barnacles; their sexuality has gone haywire, all the females are developing penises.

'Well there's Thatcherism for you,' said Dora. 'In the Enterprise Society we'll all grow penises and like it.'

Outside the harbour wall slid past, bearing its red blinking light, its wartime shell holes. On the dark quay the *Douane* was the only lit building. Colin scooped papers into his briefcase. 'Well, Topsy,' he said. 'Now for the fun part.'

'Are you sure you read it right?'

Dora tilted Rolande's map at an angle. In the Place de la République ravens ganged up in the eaves of the church; it was midnight, the streets were empty and echoing. 'We could always walk round one more time.'

The duty-free bag clinked as Colin set it down on the bench. He lit a cigarette. 'I suppose this is where they shot them,' he said.

In Spain or Italy there would have been a photograph pressed behind glass and fading like flowers, but the plaque on the wall was plain and said merely:

Mireille Bastide, Héroïne de la Résistance.

'Look at this,' said Colin. 'Someone's been at it.' There were diagonal scorings on the greened bronze, quite deep. His finger sought out letters, deciphered a word. '*Collaboratrice*', he read.

'That's horrible,' said Dora. 'That's really horrible.'

Colin had pulled the velvet curtain as far as it would go but half of the window remained uncovered. Across the narrow street, framed in the lit window of the Hotel Clemenceau, a woman in waitress's black removed a white apron small as a lace hand-kerchief. The woman leaned on the window ledge and threw a cigarette out, talking all the time to an unseen listener. Her face was in shadow but he imagined that she would be blonde. Her hands smoothed her skirt, her hands sat on her hips. They fluttered up, angry and beseeching. They held themselves palms up, an offering. Then, defeated, they composed themselves, settling mute and flat against her thighs. It was a scene of such concentrated eroticism — the shutters framing the window, a wisp of curtain, a dim light bulb — that he felt the hairs rise on the back of his neck. I'm in France, he thought, that's the trouble: it's like one big movie. Close up of Jeanne Moreau on a telephone, Miles Davis playing, her drooped mouth entreating. Words you couldn't hear but you could imagine the plot: adultery, betrayal, murder in some purring lift or sixties apartment block. Long red fingernails winding in the telephone cord. He dodged back behind the velvet curtain. 'Do you think she saw us,' he said.

Dora was standing on a chair trying to tack a bath towel over the bare half of the window. 'The Gestapo had their headquarters there in the Occupation. Or so Rolande said. They interrogated the Canadians in the bank on the corner.'

'Don't tell me that,' Colin groaned. 'I can do without that.'

In her stocking feet Dora stood wondering where to hang up her skirt. Colin was already in bed, spectacles parked on the orange box that served as a bedside table, eyes fixed short-sightedly on the ceiling. Her cap in its shell-shaped box lay at the bottom of her holdall and she knew she should be sensible and ask, or simply place it beside his spectacles and see, but she just kept standing there and couldn't face it.

Usually you use the sheath till it dies down, the doctor had said. But honestly we don't know how effective that is. Can't you get your boyfriend to ask the consultant? Get him to really pester.

Dora liked this woman with her pony-tail and her wrinkly laugh. He can't abide the sheath, she complained, he just can't manage, it's hopeless. It wasn't as if they hadn't tried. In the beginning, sensibly and doggedly. Tried for weeks, tried all sorts of little tricks, but Colin's body wouldn't be fooled. Another man (she couldn't help thinking wistfully of Rick) might have blown the thing up like a balloon and batted it round the bedroom. But not Colin. Colin saw the little bag as a personal attack. Colin lay face down and looked at failure, a future of impotence, a long grey road which sloped all the way down to the Millenium. Then there was the night when Thatcher in a chaste blue suit ascended a Busby Berkeley staircase to heaven. This was the Grand Hotel, this was the return to Brighton, this was hubris. This was the night they threw dishtowels at the television and finally gave up on Durex.

The doctor grinned sympathetically. In any case it sounds as if rubber gloves might be more appropriate. Dora was miserable but what could you do but laugh. Why not a wet-suit, they agreed. Or a mask. Honestly you couldn't do anything these days. Aids, listeria, salmonella.

Dora was beginning to feel silly standing there in her black suspender belt. 'I love French hotel rooms,' she said determinedly. She thought of peeling bluebell wallpaper, hard white cigarette-shaped bolsters, the fluorescent strip light over the bathroom mirror which made you look so golden. She thought of the hotel room in Apt where she and Rick had clowned at the mirror in their cropped identical bleached-out hair. Franz and Mitzi. Fritz and Helga. Adolf and Eva if it came to that: if you looked like the Hitler Youth, they agreed, no wonder hitching was hard. An egg had fallen out of Rick's pack, leaving albumen smears on the chenille bedspread. We'll have to own up, Rick fretted, scrubbing uselessly: he'd always been afraid of land-ladies. What? Dora hooted. You know what she'll say. Mon Dieu les Anglais with their lame excuses. Later they'd gone out for a fifty franc meal and when they came back there was a terrible snorting noise, like catarrhal breathing or the strangled suction of a blocked drain. Rick put his ear to the water pipes while Dora checked the lampshades for fat apopleptic moths. The noise seemed to come from the bedside cabinet. She'd hidden behind Rick while he wrenched open the drawer. Then, peering round his shoulder, she blushed, she fell about. Christ, said Rick, it must have turned itself on. For there was the Bible, all atremble, and there was her vibrator nuzzling up to it, humming away to itself.

The suspender belt had left a little red welt around her waist. Dora slipped under the duvet and found a place waiting in the crook of Colin's arm. She'd loved Rick, his slanted eyes the colour of honey; they'd had fun, fierce crackling laughter like lies. He

hadn't been free, but there you go. That's what happened when
you didn't think, just got lonely and lurched at someone. Colin,
on the other hand, was definitely free. Well, not married, at least.
Something which her therapist considered a great advance. Dora
smiled sideways at Colin. Patience and prudence had never been
her strong points but this time she was determined to learn. She
stroked a finger down his nose. 'Nice,' she said. Beyond his
profile was a plain white wall but she could just about imagine
the bluebells.

'So o o,' said Colin, and threw himself on top of her. His face
was guilty and grinning. 'So where's your cap, then?'

'But but but,' said Dora, as he fluttered his eyes shut. She
watched his mouth hesitate and talk. She'd seen him on
television recently, some media programme: he'd managed a
whole interview without opening his eyes once. It was rather like
a game her father had played when she was little: first he'd tug on
his tongue to shut his eyes, then he'd pop his eyes open and the
tough big tongue would disappear. In out, open shut. Cause and
effect. She was thoroughly foxed, torn between laughter and tears
at this abominable choice, one or the other when she wanted the
lot.

'He said it's okay. Less than 10 per cent of men get it from their
girlfriends.'

Dora thought Colin looked awfully pleased with himself. She
tried to turn the equation on its head and, failing, hugged him
gratefully. Okay so she was a risk but one which he was willing to
take. 'Maybe we should throw a party,' she said 'for the medical
advisors.' Gynaecologists, epidemiologists, psychotherapists.
They'd all stand round in a circle with cherries in their martinis
and nurturing permissive smiles. Thinking about it, Dora's belly
grew big and warm with anticipation. She cupped her hand
under Colin's balls. 'Little baby factories,' she said affectionately.
She thought of all the tiny fish and giggled. 'I'll have five or ten
little babies please.' She wanted to put her tongue in Colin's
mouth so that he would open his eyes and they would be happy

rocking together in the big white bed in the unfinished white room.

Colin reared up above her and opened his eyes narrowly. 'As long as they're fantasy ones.'

'Spoilsport,' said Dora.

Dora went to sleep reminding herself of a door. A locked Dora, blocked and barred. And now she dreams of a bar-room, a bar-room on a lit and marvellously promising island she sailed to. The bar-room is full of lump-shaped wooden people who appear to be a new line in pub decor, like horse-brasses or artificial rubber plants. The wooden people don't speak, just sit there in sociable postures creating an ambience. Everything is heavy and brown and begins with D., and Dora's throat constricts. She breathes shallowly, squeezing the dream out. Something wooden and brown is about to emerge from her thighs, something shaped like a big erect penis, an enormous Durex, or else a beautiful big aeroplane ascending at a forty-five degree angle, and maybe they can both fly away, she and Colin, to a country that isn't England, fly to Canada on a beautiful big aeroplane.

Colin stirs in his sleep, for Colin is afraid of flying. He grinds his fillings: grind grind. He is grinding himself to the ground. Colin dreams of escape too; he dreams of driving with Dora between thick box hedges which have been trimmed into exactly perfect walls, but then a cheeky bird sticks its head through the hedge and says cuckoo and when they arrive at the château he's dying for a piss but there's a baby floating in the toilet bowl, at which point he lets out a startled snore which wakens Dora entirely.

'What?' said Dora, as Colin came instantly alert.

'What's that?' Outside on the landing there was a low growl, snuffling. 'I thought I heard feet.'

'I expect it's the dog. Rolande says there's an Alsatian which pees on the stairs. Relax,' said Dora.

Colin tried to. He arched his stiff back, cracking the vertebrae loudly. 'I don't like Alsatians,' he grumbled. 'Gestapo dogs. All these great gnashing teeth.'

'You can talk,' said Dora.

Behind Colin's eyelids all was sensation; immense flowery smells of her hair. He lay prone, wondering what day it was, and whether he had to give a lecture. Then he remembered, and his morning prick grew sleepily large as he imagined Dora under him, her odd greedy willingness; when he entered her she would be wet and alarming and delicious. He felt her hand move lightly down his spine, giving permission. In here it was froggy and dark, like the old reservoir pipe he used to crawl into, full of couch grass and coke cans and shrunken rejected conkers. Hang a sack over each end and you had an exciting echoey prison. He was eating gobstoppers in the dimness, he was a little boy fat with secret eating, a fat little boy waddling beside his mother. Then one day his will grew huge and dark and set on transformation, although this he told to no one but the earwigs. The prognosis wasn't hopeful. He practised every day, the weight peeling off him, the waste-ground his pitch and the disused pipe his narrow goal. Took a year to make it to the school team, football boots strung around his neck and dancing on their laces, now he knew that when he really put his mind to something there was no stopping him.

Around ten the sun came in briefly above the sagging curtain and they made love again and Dora in hiding watched enviously as Colin disappeared and returned to her. In the Hotel Clemenceau someone creaked the shutters open and shook a duvet out of a window. Under her the sheet was soaked, he couldn't say she hadn't enjoyed it. She imagined hanging it out of the window like bridal linen, the besmeared obligatory proof.

When she got up and sat on the bidet she remembered that it was Saturday and Colin was right and she had to be good. Out in the streets it was raining lightly and the housewives of the town flew from Charcuterie to Boulangerie, greeting one another. There was a smell of the sea, coffee, drains, hot pastry, boiling *pieds de porc*, roast almonds, diesel, and confectioner's custard. Dora bought bread and milk and *café moulu*, and a big fish whose name she couldn't remember. She burst into the flat feeling devoted but Colin was already up, doing Tai Chi in slow circles around the laid kitchen table. 'I was going to bring you breakfast in bed,' she complained, and Colin looked at her. Colin shut his eyes and smiled his dour Trintignant smile. 'Oh shit,' she said, 'You're the boss, of course.'

So there was the park, with its memorial to the Canadians, and there was the beach, a steep shelve of clackety pebbles with shuttered hotels and February rain slanting in hard from the mushroom-coloured sky above the Channel. Dimly across the bay Dora could see Pourville, where the Surrealists, Rolande said, had summered; that was where they were going tomorrow; a real country walk for once, because it would be Sunday so Colin couldn't argue.

Colin's ungloved hands were red with cold and his sleeves were stained with soaked dark patches. They huddled together under a smallish black umbrella, their long dark coats reaching almost to their ankles: *Un Homme et Une Femme* Dora said, but Colin hadn't seen it and anyway in the movie she would have been taller so that when he put his arms round her neck and touched his forehead to hers he'd appear quite small and vulnerable and needing her.

'My shoes are soaked through,' she said. 'I thought you didn't like the elements.' Colin shook the drips from his hair and went on walking. His face was secretive with glee and adventures. Dora was mystified. It was only a bloody beach, after all, she could hardly see the excitement in that.

'Shut up, Topsy,' Colin put his arm round her waist and tugged her on into the rain. Behind his glasses his eyes crowed at her. 'You're supposed to be the outward bound freak, remember.'

In the bathroom mirror Colin examined the broken stump of his filling. Luckily it was quite far back, almost invisible really, if he smiled on the other side of his mouth. Kate and Lilian, bless their little cotton socks, had clear cruel categories for age groups. From twenty to thirty were the Middle Aged, then came the Wrinkles, and finally the Crumblies, who were utterly beyond the pale. He lathered his face and grimaced horribly at it. Well, he'd got used to being a Wrinkly but it looked as if it was Crumbly time.

In the kitchen he watched Dora wrap the big fish in foil and set the oven control somewhere between *soufflés* and *petits pigeons*. 'There!' she said, drying her hands on her jeans and looking at him expectantly. Colin felt exhausted. It was as if every little event of the day had to be served up with this relentless demand for congratulations. He drank some wine and stood at the window, snapping his fingers to Youssou N'Dour. The music was magic and he willed her to listen. If only she'd relax. Swim with it, let the sweet currents carry her. He circled his hips lazily but the rest of him was frowsty and anxious and wouldn't be convinced. A memory nagged at him: midwinter, near Christmas. Dora arriving at the flat in the long dark coat. She'd come racing up the stairs with that vigilant smile, and before he'd had time to open his mouth she was scolding: Hey. *Hey.* You haven't admired my new raincoat. Yet in the meantime, what did she ever find to admire about him?

Psychotherapy 2.

'But I can tell as soon as I go into her flat, sometimes it's like she's wearing a big placard which says hands off bad boy don't touch, a peck on the cheek if I'm lucky, her hips held stiff and away, except that one time she stopped smoking and said she was hooked, had to have a substitute, then she was softer her whole face changed and she had to have me, soft in black sweater and smooth suspenders, I laid my head in her lap and her thighs were blissful smooth above stockings so wet we hardly made it to the bedroom, her tight skirt crunched up, throwing her shoes off, a serious fuck with the suspender belt still digging into her waist, a serious fuck I was aching to take all the way thinking maybe this was the time she'd come and I start to concentrate, lose it, start in again, sometimes I have to draw away quickly afterwards, stop touching in case I burst or burn because what does it mean if she doesn't, if I can't reassure or excite her enough and she can't let go, won't take the pleasure be vulnerable, maybe let me give and give her the pleasure, the pleasure she gives without being vulnerable which makes me vulnerable, deep pleasure of mouth belly bum knees against her, arms around me tight and sighs and eyes closed smiling not criticizing, soft dark cloudy little wet curled hairs, she's so wet I give myself up inside her dissolving nowhere, the smell of her hair, bum sticking out at me so you can't help asking why she doesn't, it's like a slap there's no pleasing her although she cries and says there is, but if someone loves you if you excite them don't they dissolve, how else do you know, what does she expect me to think, either she's holding back refusing or she doesn't want me maybe never did always refused, refuse I'm just, only, to her, she's in apron, back turned, stocking seams, emptying the refuse and you can't ask for anything can't please can't do anything for her, look after her or anything much, and you go on hoping like a dumb animal speaking tongues she won't listen to, she blocks up her ears, the open pink ear of her body that opens me and I talk to in conversation, communication pouring into her, fingers tongue but she's tangled up in head-words, past and all that refuse, it frightens me, her anger tears lashing at me and how she topples into her absence, and oh I can talk all right, talk till the cows come home theory analysis semiotics the lot up to my bloody eyes in it is that what she wants, nothing much, nothing's ever good enough, the body I live in aching out in the cold rain and grey not touching, my hand small in hers like anything she didn't know was there, like shopping or fishbones, my skin a brawl of sadness, do I have to ask for everything, plead, my head on the chopping block, should anyone have to ask for everything when I give give and she doesn't hear me, it's like music on a radio no one's listening to in a shut room powerless vibrations on the airwaves she just keeps out.'

The fish had come out of the oven and Dora was flirting. 'But haven't you ever been in love,' she demanded. 'You mean to say you've never been in love.' She waved her wine glass in the air and her eyes sparkled.

Colin chewed a green bean, keeping it well away from the cavity. 'At 17, I guess, if you could call it that. I was fucking out of my head.' It wasn't an experience he cared to recall. She'd carried him in her pocket, he'd never known another human being could inflict such pain.

Dora looked eager. 'But that's what it's about, isn't it?'

'Shut up, Topsy,' he ordered, remembering that he had a right to. 'What it was *about* was tearing down the M1 every weekend in a clapped-out car with my stomach in knots. What it was *about* was having to stay stoned out of my head for a year afterwards . . .'

Dora leaned forward. 'But since?' she insisted. 'Never since?'

'Good fish,' said Colin, swallowing. 'I'm telling you, once was enough.'

'Oh!' Dora cried. 'I don't think I like you any more, I really don't.'

'Ha,' said Colin, eyeing her bleakly. 'So you did once, did you?' He reached for the cognac. The guilt would come later, but for the moment it was gratifying, the way her smile froze open in an O of surprise.

When they were in bed Dora reached out for him. He felt her melt for a moment and his hopes soared, but then she shut her eyes again and fought God knows what dark battles on the inside of her eyelids, and they were back to square one or worse.

'How's your back?' Dora enquired afterwards.

'So-so,' said Colin, who felt as if he had had an amputation. He lay in his own sweat, wishing and hopeless. She was being too kind and he wanted to cry. Giving was powerful and so was his pleasure but she made it so plain that she wouldn't take. 'Maybe if you sat on it,' he muttered. 'Sometimes the pressure helps.'

Dora sat on the base of Colin's spine, separating vertebrae, smoothing muscle spasm away, shaking it off the ends of her fingers. Underneath her Colin groaned. 'Harder. More weight.'

'I feel like a torturer,' she said, as Colin's back arched up at her, armoured, cracking. Awful racking noises of punishment. She said that hurt to cure hurt couldn't be right, she was convinced of it. She said there was an image missing, a word unsaid, trapped in there like fluid in a blister. When she shut her eyes she saw the word surrounded in tears. She kneaded her thumbs strongly along the shallows of the longissimus dorsi and tried to remember the French for 'to gut'. Behind closed lids she watched her fingers run down the bared spine of the mackerel/hake/ mullet, nails stripping out the blood vessels and the nerve cord in its transparent conduit, the cold tap flushing out all sorts of little sacs. Fish scales glittering silver on her hands. Colin groaned again once and was silent. Under her his muscles yielded a little, then balked. 'Stop resisting,' she ordered.

When the pain went it was replaced by an insecure floaty sensation and Colin was frightened and laughed. 'No armour, no character,' he joked, 'Just as I always suspected.' Dora slid off his back and lay crushed up against him and he didn't want her to go away, not to the bidet or anywhere, not for one moment. He tucked himself into her back until he fitted and sneaked his hands round her breasts and lay there almost crooning with pleasure. In the image his mother had worn a nightdress and his finger was bandaged but the feeling was the same. He wasn't sure such depths of pleasure should be permitted.

In the morning Colin rolled off Dora and put his head in his hands.

'Don't sulk,' said Dora, who was almost there and in any case it was Sunday. 'Help me.' Last night when she'd brushed her hair in the dark the sparks had flown, she was constantly ready to ignite if only he would let her. Down in the bed their fingers nudged each other. She was warm, wet, liking his touch better than hers. She let out a little moan of delight.

'Mmm?' said Colin hopefully. His face had a blindfold look, like someone at a party they never wanted to have.

'Mm,' breathed Dora, guilt-stricken.

Colin was staring at her left nipple. The frown deepened on his forehead. 'But don't you ever come from just fucking,' he said.

'Well,' said Dora, as her body flickered, faded, and finally stopped transmitting. 'You'd probably have to marry me.'

Colin let out a high-pitched laugh. She watched his pale spine slither out of bed. 'I think I'll just make the coffee instead.'

'Joke,' said Dora glumly to his back. But as soon as he was out of the room she got her mettle up. A few strokes and she came in a cloud of sparks and immediately felt good-humoured. She hummed the Marseillaise to her bare splayed feet. Any way you could come was the right way, so why should she let Colin put her in the wrong.

Tucking the croissants under his coat Colin dragged himself back along the Rue des Cigognes. His head was full of mud, his knees wobbled. It must be all the sex, he decided. Or else he was getting the 'flu. Passing the Hotel Clemenceau, he could hear the clink of forks. Although it was noon the day was dark and the lights were on in the dining-room. He stopped on the pavement to read the menu, wiping the drizzle from the glass case with his sleeve. *Crêpes de fruits de mer, quenelles de brochet*, the inevitable *moules*. The indeterminate watery sensation washed through him again, followed by a feeling that was almost like rage. The hotel loomed, its stone balconies and porticoes like massive intruders into his space. He had a sudden conviction that his spine had been replaced by a series of hollow tubes, malleable and transparent, and for a second he was convulsed, hating the world with a ravaging hatred. If anyone had jostled him at that moment he would have knocked them into the road without a thought. He put out a hand to steady himself on the metal post which supported the menu, and as he did so an image flickered through his head. Odysseus lashed to the mast, Odysseus who had asked to be. He snatched his hand away, feeling ridiculous, and began to think frantically of work. Turning his coat collar up he fled across the cobbled street to the door of the flats, hoping against hope that no one in the dining-room had seen this *type* in middle age who clung to a menu-post in the rain.

When he went into the bedroom Dora was lacing up her walking boots. 'We are going to Pourville,' she said, 'aren't we.' He drew the curtain aside to reveal the drizzle but Dora merely shrugged. 'I've got to see a gorse bush,' she announced truculently.

On the breakwater Dora threw up her arms and laughed at the crashing waves. The sea will roll us in its bones, she thought, and we will be clean and afraid. Well the poets would love her if he didn't. Eluard and Aragon and all that lot. Although he ought to. She loved herself like this, not meek and mimsy and trying hard. Colin looked cold, his odd body drawn back from the white rubble of waves. Him with his lightning-conductor umbrella, she thought. Neither wet-haired in the wind nor sea-sick with love. And then she repented and, picking up a pebble which was glassy grey and perfectly round, she put it in her pocket for him.

Colin studied the faded yellow print on the canister. *Nettoyage*, it said. *Nucléaire*, it said. He dropped it quickly and stood fretting over it for a moment, wondering if the tide had carried it from the nuclear plant along the coast. He kicked the canister angrily and watched it sail through the air and disappear behind a World War 2 bunker. A cleaning fluid that removes contamination, he thought. Who the fuck are they trying to kid?

Once upon a time the bunker must have been redoubtable, but decades and the sea had undermined its foundations, so that now it lay askew, belly-flopped astride a pebble bank, gaping and incongruous. Colin tied his muffler tighter against the wind and took a closer look. The reinforced concrete was four feet thick, but the brick cladding had been smoothed and indented by the waves until the surface looked like a shifting sea on which brick-shapes had been painted – a slippery effect which Dali might have envied but which left Colin feeling distinctly giddy. Turning his back on the wall he crouched down out of the wind and ate a chunk of the baguette which Dora had filled with *céleri rémoulade*. He smoked a cigarette, cupping it in his hand. Down by the breakers Dora appeared to be transported. Pointing in triumph at the sudden gleam of sun, she danced back up the beach towards him. 'That's our reward,' she cried. 'I told you we'd get a reward.'

Colin felt his eyes fill shockingly with tears. He forced his lips into a grin. 'Trouble with you,' he said. 'You're a megalomaniac.'

On the way back from Pourville Colin's black city shoes went careful on the cliff road. Overhead the sky piled up possibilities of thunder and the air was heavy and bristling with static. Dora was frightened. 'Look, we could hitch,' she said, as hailstones fell from a huge greenish cloud and rattled on the surface of Colin's black umbrella.

'Oh sure,' said Colin. 'Just look at us.'

'You'll see,' said Dora, sticking out her thumb. Quite soon a small Renault had drawn up and two young men in leather jackets laughed out at them: *Vous allez où?* Clearing the back seat of cassettes. The driver accelerated hard, talking rapidly over his shoulder. *Canadiens? Americains? Anglais*, okay, *d'accord*, he had worked the Bateau Sealink himself for *quelques années*. Colin chatted along affably but Dora's French had deserted her. She shut her eyes as the car screeched round the first steep bend above the town. The white slick of hail on the road was already criss-crossed by skid marks. She clutched at Colin's hand. 'Christ, we should have walked,' she said.

When they got out of the car Colin threw back his head and laughed. 'You're incredible. If it isn't lightning it's French drivers.'

In the bathroom mirror Dora looked at him with interest. His cheeks glowed, his eyes flashed, his hair stuck up in bunches round his head. 'You're all excited,' she observed. 'Maybe adventures suit you.' She had stripped off her wet jeans and now she was wearing a long pleated skirt and a pair of white football socks. 'Actually I've got no knickers on,' she confided.

'Oh don't worry,' said Colin, 'I'm going to fuck you, all right.'

Dora lay on the bed and looked down at her white socks. Okay so he was holding her hand but why was his face so far away and bolting, his mouth mutinous?

'Feel like a song?' Colin asked. His face hovered over her, a Sphinx. Propping his back against the white wall he shut his eyes and began to sing. It was a ballad from the far north, melancholy. Listening, she fancied that she could hear the yearning, for love or his mother or a fast horse or the guitar he couldn't play. Colin had perfect pitch; his mouth became round and his invisible tongue made sublime noises in the dark. Dora sniffed and dried her eyes and wondered whether to be soothed. The savage breast and so on. But surely her tears weren't so terrifying. Couldn't he see that it was only her child-self ringing to say it missed her, asking if it could come?

Two dogs, two great big dogs straining at the leash. Two dogs in a lather, aiming at him.

In the middle of the night Colin sat up straight with the breath sucked out of him. They had forgotten the bath towel and anyone could have spied in, oh la la les Anglais with le dirty weekend. He lay rigid, cradling his genitals with his hand. Across the street a woman stood behind the window staring out. Rain ran down the window or perhaps it was tears. She pressed her hands against the glass, her hands pleaded, her hands beckoned into the dark where he was. A bare light bulb swung in the room behind her. He saw her mouth move, soundless: murder was what she was talking about but he didn't want to know. Sweat cooled on his bare chest. He switched the bedside light on and Dora blinked. 'Did you scream or something?' she asked sleepily.

Resistance 2.

She'll be wearing a uniform, something that looks like a uniform, some sort of suit, something mannish which gives the same effect. She won't have a blouse underneath, though, just these sharp square shoulders and angular lapels against clear pale skin. In a time when other women pencilled pretend seams up the back of their legs, this one wears sheer silk stockings and ankle-strap shoes, shoes for fucking. And because of how the English prisoner's lying – face down on a long table, hands manacled to the table legs – you know he can only see the slim calves, the shoes, the hem of her narrow skirt. The woman's head is bent close to his, her hair brushes his ear as she whispers: *Un petit mot, camarade.* Just a little word. The Englishman fights back the tears which rise unbidden to his eyes. Just a little word and then you can sleep. White fingers with their long crimson nails stroking his sweat-damp hair, his face filthy with sweat and blood, and oh how badly he wants to sleep, just a little word and he can sleep deep in her arms like an angel while her cloudy hair billows out around him. A bare light bulb swings in a draught, and the sharp shadow-shoulders of the woman sway back and forth, back and forth. He digs his nails into his palms and bites back the word. In the vaults of the *Banque* day and night merge into that staring white light, and again and again he falls out into the moon, flashback to the parachute billowing around him like a great green cloud as he circles in the moonlight, a perfect target until the thick hedge crashes into the small of his back and breaks into cushions of leaves, tumbling him upside down so that he hangs helpless in his harness, and there's the statue of a woman – white, Greek – a formal garden, and silhouettes of château turrets, and below him his blacked-out face reflected, mouth gaping among the reddish lazy shapes of carp.

And then the woman moving like a wraith, her light raincoat separating itself from the white outline of the statue, the knife cutting him down. Her hands run over him, strong hands which search for broken bones, dark eyes under the tilted beret which smile when she finds none, and it's a sad smile, a sensual smile, a smile full of mystery.

In the morning they drink bitter coffee in the café on the *quai* and wait for the rendezvous. Outside small boats unload the night's catch, barrels of silver sardines which shiver and twitch, live lobsters and crabs and mackerel whose dead bared teeth protrude through the slatted boxes. The Frenchwoman gets up and goes to the telephone and her mouth droops as she speaks into the receiver, her mouth is red and her eyes are grey and sad and her lashes are black as black. When she returns to her seat her fingertips tap the table and her eyes flicker restlessly round the café, watching. At a corner table a workman frowns at his ration card; behind the bar the *patron* rubs sleep from his eyes and sells cigarettes to a man in a slouch hat. A clerk in pince-nez sorts coins out of a threadbare purse, a woman with a voluminous chignon smokes cigarette after cigarette, a blue-overalled youth delivers bread. Any one of them, the Englishman knows, could be the informer who has penetrated the network, the traitor London has sent him to unmask. But although he watches the French-woman's face for a sign, a flicker of recognition, her sad eyes betray nothing.

Soon the café is full of steam and noise and outside the *quai* disappears behind misted windows. Fishermen, hollow-eyed from the night's work, chaff each other over glasses of *rouge*. Suddenly coins clatter on the tiled floor and the Englishman is immediately alert: the woman with the chignon has dropped her basket and is bending to retrieve its contents. And is it his imagination, or does the man in the slouch hat close his newspaper at this very moment, as if responding to a signal, and walk silently out of the café?

But now the thin man in pince-nez approaches the table and stands beside them stirring saccharine into his coffee. *Bonjour*, Mireille, he says, with a glance at the unshaven face of the Englishman opposite her. *Bonjour*, Jacques, Mireille responds, while the Englishman waits for the password. *Bonjour*, Pasteur, Jacques murmurs. Your aunt has had a good trip? Excellent, responds the Englishman. But one of our cousins was too ill to travel. Jacques' eyes glint behind the pince-nez. He will recover, *n'est-ce pas?* The Englishman shrugs. Only with treatment.

Jacques nods curtly at Mireille, who gets up and threads her way through the tables to a door marked *Toilettes*. Then he lets out his breath on a sigh. *C'est vrai, quand-même*. And then his chair scrapes back and he's pulling the Englishman to his feet, for suddenly there's the screech of brakes outside, and heavy boots echo on the cobbles. There's a lull in the café noise, someone curses and spits on the floor. The Boches, Jacques hisses. We've been betrayed.

And now in the hard light the Englishman sees again the drooping red mouth speaking into the telephone, the drooping mouth which whispers into his ear: Just a little word, comrade, or those pigs will hurt you badly. And he digs his nails into his palms as the days and the words billow out around him like a parachute: ciphers, the disposition of networks, codes for supply drops, derailments. Everything he knows about the infrastructure of British Intelligence. Then, and only then, will they be satisfied, will they grant him the peace at the foot of the wall after the firing squad has returned to barracks, the one freedom which remains in the fate of the spy. He gathers his breath, self, his heart and soul ache with the effort of resisting. *Jamais*, he spits.

Mireille sighs. Her red fingernails tap the table. Then they trail caressingly down his back, delicate as the tail of a whip. Outside a German guard dog barks and is silenced by a brusque command. Mireille says something in German, in a wistful tone, and he could almost weep as the whispering fingernails retreat and he waits for the other fingers, the steel fingers of the enema, the shame flooding through him, the electrodes, the days which billow out around him, the bath-tub on the edge of which Mireille sits like a mirage, swinging her silk-stockinged legs, the bathroom with its vanity mirror and the vase of impossible white roses, the sound of cigarette lighters and laughter, the smell of pocked flesh burning. He digs his nails into his palms to the sound of his own distant shouting as the days billow out around him and he memorizes the exact proportions of his cell, 6 metres by 4, the barred window at a height of 5 metres and a half, the number of bricks in the wall 36 squared times 18 squared, the number of bars in the window, the number of pull-ups which delineate the days, nights, the dawns grey and translucent as her eyes, the white thighs they tell her to show him, the red fingernails lifting the short skirt, the frill of lace, the brutal fingers spreading the thighs to show him the secrets under the silk, the things they promised he could do to that lovely treacherous body, the mouth which whispers to him that the Boches are holding her mother and she is powerless, she is their puppet, she must do anything they say and she stands there with the whip held loosely across her naked breasts and of course it is as he always knew, the Gestapo will crush and humiliate, they will make you beg for your mother and they will promise her to you in the end you will believe their promises and see her in their faces and hear her soft voice in theirs and you will kiss her hand for joy . . . but as the metal pincers grip at him he knows there is no escape, none, none, no escape and he's falling into darkness silhouetted against the moon as the room billows out around him.

And now dawn comes, dawn creeps across the floor of the cell where the Englishman lies bloody but unbeaten. Slowly he wakes, painfully his eyes focus on the wretched bed in the corner, while in another bed with snowy pillows marred only by a faint smear of crimson lipstick Mireille B. stirs in the arms of a German lieutenant, and stretches, and smiles. Slowly he crawls, agonizingly, towards the bed, and extricates the sharpened wire which he has concealed under the straw pallet, and hides it in his hand. Then with almost his last strength he taps a farewell message on the wall. In the next cell Jacques, receiving it, strikes the wall with his fist. No, *mon brave*, I beg you. But the

Englishman steels his resolve. Carefully, like a surgeon, he opens the vein in his left wrist, then, more clumsily, his right. And as the blood first seeps, then pulses, he feels the walls settling, the walls and days and nights no longer a delirium as his cell narrows and his skin narrows to fit him and he laughs in his bitterness and pride thinking of the faces of the Gestapo swine when they find his body narrow and cold with its secrets intact, and as his consciousness ebbs the smile fixes on his bruised unrecognizable face, and all along the corridors rings the cry which Jacques has begun and his comrades have taken up, and the guards in their barracks hear it, and the officers in their bath-tubs, and the hotel cooks in their kitchen, and Mireille in her soft bed, Mireille who buries her head in the snowy pillow and weeps for shame: *A bas l'infâme esclavage Hitlérien! Vive la Résistance!*

Talk to me, Dora thought, as the boat left the harbour. Colin's face was blurred with tiredness, his eyes red. She struck a dead match and cursed. Later the boat kicked and kicked like a foetus and she got sick again and lay flat and talked to herself sorrowfully in her own aching belly-head, pity, pity, and she held Colin's hand and that was enough, cow-comfort, animal, that was far better than words.

On the train she watched Colin puzzle over his diary. She ate French bread and *chèvre* to stave off England and laughed at the crumbs which fell on her coat. Why can't he just relax, she thought impatiently. Already the weekend was a warm store in the belly of the past but there was no peace on Colin's face. He was muttering about tonight, sorry, lectures to prepare; his eyes were closed, his brow was in agony. 'Look, don't worry,' she said, to prove that he wasn't disappointing her. Well, they'd had fun, hadn't they. She settled on the idea with relief. This is what they'd say to each other at the station barrier, an intimate consensus of two in the Victoria mêlée.

The train passed Gatwick and a single thin tree which sparkled with white blossom. Remembering the pebble, she dropped it into his palm and felt tender, thinking of his busy week and how he would carry it in his pocket to remind him.

Then London was all around them, and people were flinging open the carriage doors. Colin shouldered his holdall with a sigh. Dora took this to indicate nostalgia and, encouraged, turned her face up for a kiss and waited. 'Straight back to the grind, then,' said Colin, throwing the pebble gaily up and catching it. Then, with a smile that was almost rakish, he popped it into his mouth.

Well, if that's the best he can do, Dora said to herself, as he went off sucking it.

The Fair Floo'er o' Northumberland

O the Provost's ae dochter was walkin' her way
O but her love it was easy won
When she spied a Scots prisoner makin' his main
Aye and she was the Floo'er o' Northumberland.

'Tis o gin ma lassie wid marry me
O gin her love it was easy won
I would mak her a lady o' high degree
If she'd loose me oot frae my prison sae strang.

So 'tis she's done her doon tae her faither's guid stocks
O but her love it was easy won
And she's ta'en the best keys there for mony a brave lock
For tae loose him oot frae his prison sae strang.

And 'tis she's done her doon tae her faither's guid stable
O but her love it was easy won
And she's stolen the best horse that was baith fleet and able
For tae carry them back tae bonnie Scotland.

But as they were a 'ridin across yon Scots muir
He cried o but your love it was easy won
Get ye doon frae my horse, ye're a brazen-faced hoor
Although ye're the Floo'er o' Northumberland.

O 'tis cook in your kitchen I shairly will be
O but my love it was easy won
For I canny gae back tae my ain country
Although I'm the Floo'er o' Northumberland

O 'tis cook in my kitchen ye canny weel be
O but your love it was easy won
For my lady she willnae hae servants like thee
And ye'll hae tae gae back tae Northumberland

For 'tis I hae a wife in my ain country
O but your love it was easy won
And I canny dae naethin wi a lassie like thee
And you'll hae tae gae back tae Northumberland.

(Scots traditional, abridged)

HUMILITY

KATHY ACKER

HUMILITY

Dead Doll

HUMILITY

IN ANY SOCIETY BASED ON CLASS, HUMILIATION IS A POLITICAL REALITY. HUMILIATION IS ONE METHOD BY WHICH POLITICAL POWER IS TRANS-FORMED INTO SOCIAL OR PERSONAL RELATIONSHIPS. THE PERSONAL INTERIORIZATION OF THE PRACTICE OF HUMILIATION IS CALLED *HUMILITY*

CAPITOL IS AN ARTIST WHO MAKES DOLLS. MAKES, DAMAGES, TRANSFORMS, SMASHES. ONE OF HER DOLLS IS A WRITER DOLL. THE WRITER DOLL ISN'T VERY LARGE AND IS ALL HAIR, HORSE-MANE HAIR, RAT FUR, DIRTY HUMAN HAIR, PUSSY.

ONE NIGHT CAPITOL GAVE THE FOLLOWING SCENARIO TO HER WRITER DOLL:

As a child in sixth grade in a North American school, won first prize in a poetry contest.

In late teens and early twenties, entered New York City poetry world. Prominent Black Mountain poets, mainly male, taught or attempted to teach her that a writer becomes a writer when and only when he finds his own voice.

CAPITOL DIDN'T MAKE ANY AVANT-GARDE POET DOLLS.

Since wanted to be a writer, tried to find her own voice. Couldn't. But still loved to write. Loved to play with language. Language was material like clay or paint. Loved to play with verbal material, build up slums and mansions, demolish banks and half-rotten buildings, even buildings which she herself had constructed, into never-before-seen, even unseeable, jewels.

To her, every word wasn't only material in itself, but also sent out like beacons other words. *Blue* sent out *heaven* and *The Virgin*. Material is rich. I didn't create language, writer thought. Later she would think about ownership and copyright. I'm constantly being given language. Since this language-world is rich and always changing, flowing, when I write, I enter a world which has complex relations and is, perhaps, illimitable. This world both represents and is human history, public memories and private memories turned public, the records and actualizations of human intentions. This world is more than life and death, for here life and death conjoin. I can't make language, but in this world, I can play and be played.

So where is 'my voice'?

Wanted to be a writer.

Since couldn't find 'her voice', decided she'd first have to learn what a Black Mountain poet meant by 'his voice'. What did he do when he wrote?

A writer who had found his own voice presented a viewpoint. Created meaning. The writer took a certain amount of language, verbal material, forced that language to stop radiating in multiple, even unnumerable directions, to radiate in only one direction so there could be his meaning.

The writer's voice wasn't exactly this meaning. The writer's voice was a process, how he had forced that language to obey him, his will. The writer's voice is the voice of the writer-as-God.

Writer thought, don't want to be God; have never wanted to be God. All these male poets want to be the top poet, as if, since they can't be a dictator in the political realm, can be dictator of this world.

Want to play. Be left alone to play. Want to be a sailor who journeys at every edge and even into the unknown. See strange sights, see. If I can't keep on seeing wonders, I'm in prison. Claustrophobia's sister to my worst nightmare: lobotomy, the total loss of perceptual power, of seeing new. If had to force language to be uni-directional, I'd be helping my own prison to be constructed.

There are enough prisons outside, outside language.

Decided, no. Decided that to find her own voice would be negotiating against her joy. That's what the culture seemed to be trying to tell her to do.

Wanted only to write. Was writing. Would keep on writing without finding 'her own voice'. To hell with the Black Mountain poets even though they had taught her a lot.

Decided that since what she wanted to do was just to write, not to find her own voice, could and would write by using anyone's voice, anyone's text, whatever materials she wanted to use.

Had a dream while waking that was running with animals. Wild horses, leopards, red fox, kangaroos, mountain lions, wild dogs. Running over rolling hills. Was able to keep up with the animals and they accepted her.

Wildness was writing and writing was wildness.

Decision not to find this own voice but to use and be other, multiple, even innumerable, voices led to two other decisions.

There were two kinds of writing in her culture: good literature and schlock. Novels which won literary prizes were good literature; science fiction and horror novels, pornography were schlock. Good literature concerned important issues, had a high moral content, and, most important, was written according to well-established rules of taste, elegance, and conservatism. Schlock's content was sex horror violence and other aspects of human existence abhorrent to all but the lowest of the low, the socially and morally unacceptable. This trash was made as quickly as possible, either with no regard for the regulations of politeness or else with regard to the crudest, most vulgar techniques possible. Well-educated, intelligent and concerned people read good literature. Perhaps because the masses were gaining political therefore economic and social control, not only of literary production, good literature was read by an élite diminishing in size and cultural strength.

Decided to use or to write both good literature and schlock. To mix them up in terms of content and formally.

Offended everyone.

Writing in which all kinds of writing mingled seemed, not immoral, but amoral, even to the masses. Played in every playground she found; no one can do that in a class or hierarchical society.

(In literature classes in university, had learned that anyone can say or write anything about anything if he or she does so cleverly enough. That cleverness, one of the formal rules of good literature, can be a method of social and political manipulation. Decided to use language stupidly.) In order to use and be other voices as stupidly as possible, decided to copy down simply other texts.

Copy them down while, maybe, mashing them up because wasn't going to stop playing in any playground. Because loved wildness.

Having fun with texts is having fun with everything and everyone. Since didn't have one point of view or centralized perspective, was free to find out how the texts she used and was worked. In their contexts which were (parts of) culture.

Liked best of all mushing up texts.

Began constructing her first story by placing mashed-up texts by and about Henry Kissinger next to *True Romance* texts. What was the true romance of America? Changed these *True Romance* texts only by heightening the sexual crudity of their style. Into this mush, placed four pages out of Harold Robbins', one of her heroes, newest hottest bestsellers. Had first made Jacqueline Onassis the star of Robbins' text.

Twenty years later, a feminist house republished the last third of the novel in which this mash occurred.

CAPITOL MADE A FEMINIST PUBLISHER DOLL EVEN THOUGH, BECAUSE SHE WASN'T STUPID, SHE KNEW THAT THE FEMINIST PUBLISHING HOUSE WAS ACTUALLY LOTS OF DOLLS. THE FEMINIST PUBLISHER DOLL AS A BEAUTIFUL WOMAN IN ST LAURENT DRESS. CAPITOL, PERHAPS OUT OF PERVERSITY,

REFRAINED FROM USING HER USUAL CHEWED UP CHEWING GUM, HALF-
DRIED FLECKS OF NAIL POLISH AND BITS OF HER OWN BODY THAT HAD
SOMEHOW FALLEN AWAY.

Republished the text containing the Harold Robbins' mush next
to a text she had written only seventeen years ago. In this second
text, the only one had ever written without glopping up hacking
into and rewriting other texts (appropriating), had tried to
destroy literature or what she as a writer was supposed to write by
making characters and a story that were so stupid as to be almost
non-existent. Ostensibly, the second text was a porn book. The
pornography was almost as stupid as the story. The female
character had her own name.

Thought just after had finished writing this, here is a conventional novel. Perhaps, here is 'my voice'. Now I'll never again
have to make up a bourgeois novel.

Didn't.

The feminist publisher informed her that this second text was
her most important because here she had written a treatise on
female sexuality.

Since didn't believe in arguing with people, wrote an introduction to both books in which stated that her only interest in
writing was in copying down other people's texts. Didn't say
liked messing them up because was trying to be polite. Like the
English. Did say had no interest in sexuality or in any other
content.

CAPITOL MADE A DOLL WHO WAS A JOURNALIST. CAPITOL LOVED MAKING
DOLLS WHO WERE JOURNALISTS. SOMETIMES SHE MADE THEM OUT OF THE
NEWSPAPERS FOUND IN TRASHCANS ON THE STREETS. SHE KNEW THAT LOTS
OF CATS INHABITED TRASHCANS. THE PAPERS SAID RATS CARRY DISEASES.
SHE MADE THIS JOURNALIST OUT OF THE FINGERNAILS SHE OBTAINED BY
HANGING AROUND THE TRASHCANS IN THE BACK LOTS OF LONDON
HOSPITALS. HAD PENETRATED THESE BACK LOTS WITH THE HOPE OF
MEETING MEAN OLDER MEN BIKERS. FOUND LOTS OF OTHER THINGS

THERE. SINCE, TO MAKE THE JOURNALIST, SHE MOLDED THE FINGERNAILS
TOGETHER WITH SUPERGLUE AND, BEING A SLOB, LOTS OF OTHER THINGS
STUCK TO THIS SUPERGLUE, THE JOURNALIST DIDN'T LOOK ANYTHING
LIKE A HUMAN BEING.

A journalist who worked on a trade publishing magazine, so the
story went, no one could remember whose story, was informed
by another woman in her office that there was a resemblance
between a section of the writer's book and Harold Robbins' work.
Most of the literati of the country in which the writer was
currently living were upper-middle-class and detested the writer
and her writing.

CAPITOL THOUGHT ABOUT MAKING A DOLL OF THIS COUNTRY, BUT
DECIDED NOT TO.

Journalist decided she had found a scoop. Phoned up the
feminist publisher to enquire about plagiarism; perhaps feminist
publisher said something wrong because then phoned up
Harold Robbins' publisher.

'Surely all art is the result of one's having been in danger, of
having gone through an experience all the way to the end, where
no one can go any further. The further one goes, the more private,
the more personal, the more singular an experience becomes,
and the thing one is making is finally, the necessary, irrepressible,
and, as nearly as possible, definitive utterance of this singularity
... Therein lies the enormous aid the work of art brings to the life
of the one who must make it ...

'So we are most definitely called upon to test and try ourselves
against the utmost, but probably we are also bound to keep
silence regarding this utmost, to beware of sharing it, of parting
with it in communication so long as we have not entered the
work of art: for the utmost represents nothing other than that
singularity in us which no one would or even should understand,
and which must enter into the work as such ...' Rilke to Cézanne.

CAPITOL MADE A PUBLISHER LOOK LIKE SAM PECKINPAH. THOUGH SHE HAD
NO IDEA WHAT SAM PECKINAPH LOOKED LIKE. HAD LOOKED LIKE? SHE
TOOK A HOWDY DOODY DOLL AND AN ALFRED E NEUMAN DOLL AND
MASHED THEM TOGETHER, THEN MADE THIS CONGLOMERATE INTO AN
AMERICAN OFFICER IN THE MEXICAN-AMERICAN WAR. ACTUALLY SEWED,
SHE HATED SEWING, OR WHEN SHE BECAME TIRED OF SEWING, GLUED
TOGETHER WITH HER OWN TWO HANDS, JUST AS THE EARLY AMERICAN
PATRIOT WIVES USED TO DO FOR THEIR PATRIOT HUSBANDS, A FROGGED
AND BRAIDED CAVALRY JACKET, STAINED WITH BLOOD FROM SOME FORMER
OWNERS. THEN FASHIONED A STOVEPIPE HAT OUT OF ONE SHE HAS STOLEN
FROM A BUM IN AN ECSTASY OF ART. THE HAT WAS A BIT BIG FOR THE
PUBLISHER. INSIDE A GOLD HEART, THERE SHOULD BE A PICTURE OF A
WOMAN. SINCE CAPITOL DIDN'T HAVE A PICTURE OF A WOMAN, SHE PUT IN
ONE OF HER MOTHER. SINCE SAM PECKINPAH OR HER PUBLISHER HAD SEEN
TRAGEDY, AN ARROW HANGING OUT OF THE WHITE BREAST OF A SOLDIER
NO OLDER THAN A CHILD, HORSES GONE MAD WALL-EYED MOUTHS
FROTHING AMID DUST THICKER THAN THE SMOKE OF GUNS. SHE MADE HIS
FACE FULL OF FOLDS, AN EYEPATCH OVER ONE EYE.

Harold Robbins' publisher phoned up the man who ran the
company who owned the feminist publishing company. From
now on, known as 'The Boss'. The Boss told Harold Robbins'
publisher that they have a plagiarist in their midst.

CAPITOL NO LONGER WANTED TO MAKE DOLLS. IN THE UNITED STATES
UPON SEEING THE WORK OF THE PHOTOGRAPHER ROBERT MAPPLETHORPE,
SENATOR JESSE HELMS PROPOSED AN AMENDMENT TO THE FISCAL YEAR 1990
INTERIOR AND RELATED AGENCIES BILL FOR THE PURPOSE OF PROHIBITING
'THE USE OF APPROPRIATED FUNDS FOR THE DISSEMINATION, PROMOTION,
OR PRODUCTION OF OBSCENE OR INDECENT MATERIALS OR MATERIALS
DENIGRATING A PARTICULAR RELIGION.' THREE SPECIFIC CATEGORIES OF
UNACCEPTABLE MATERIAL FOLLOWED: (1) OBSCENE OR INDECENT
MATERIALS, INCLUDING BUT NOT LIMITED TO DEPICTIONS OF SADOMA-
SOCHISM, [ALWAYS GET THAT ONE IN FIRST], HOMO-EROTICISM, THE
EXPLOITATION OF CHILDREN, OR INDIVIDUALS ENGAGED IN SEX ACTS; OR

(2) MATERIAL WHICH DENIGRATES THE OBJECTS OR BELIEFS OF THE ADHERENTS OF A PARTICULAR RELIGION OR NON-RELIGION; OR (3) MATERIAL WHICH DENIGRATES, DEBASES, OR REVILES A PERSON, GROUP, OR CLASS OF CITIZENS ON THE BASIS OF RACE, CREED, SEX, HANDICAP, AGE, OR NATIONAL ORIGIN'. IN HONOR OF JESSE HELMS, CAPITOL MADE, AS PILLOWS, A CROSS AND A VAGINA, SO THE POOR COULD HAVE SOMEWHERE TO SLEEP. SINCE SHE NO LONGER HAD TO MAKE DOLLS OR ART, BECAUSE ART IS DEAD IN THIS CULTURE, SHE SLOPPED THE PILLOWS TOGETHER WITH DEAD FLIES, WHITE FLOUR MOISTENED BY THE BLOOD SHE DREW OUT OF HER SMALLEST FINGERS WITH A PIN, AND OTHER TYPES OF GARBAGE.

Disintegration.

Feminist publisher then informed writer that the Boss and Harold Robbins' publisher had decided, due to her plagiarism, to withdraw the book from publication and to have her sign an apology to Harold Robbins which they had written. This apology would then be published in two major publishing magazines.

Ordinarily polite, told feminist publisher they could do what they wanted with their edition of her books but she wasn't going to apologize to anyone for anything, much less for twenty years of work.

Didn't have to think to herself because every square inch of her knew. For freedom. Writing must be for and must be freedom.

Feminist publisher replied that she knew writer was actually a sweet nice girl.

Asked if should tell her agent or try talking directly to Harold Robbins.

Feminist publisher replied she'd take care of everything. Writer shouldn't contact Harold Robbins because that would make everything worse.

Would, the feminist publisher asked, the writer please compose a statement for the Boss why the writer used other texts when she wrote so that the Boss wouldn't believe that she was a plagiarist.

CAPITOL MADE A DOLL WHO LOOKED EXACTLY LIKE HERSELF. IF YOU
PRESSED A BUTTON ON ONE OF THE DOLL'S CUNT LIPS THE DOLL SAID, 'I AM
A GOOD LITTLE GIRL AND DO EXACTLY AS I AM TOLD TO DO.'

Wrote:
Nobody save buzzards. Lots of buzzards here. In the
distance, lay flies and piles of shit. Herds of animals move
against the skyline like black caravans in an unknown east.
Sheep and goats. Another place, a horse is lapping the water
of a pool. Lavender and grey trees behind this black water
are leafless and spineless. As the day ends, the sun in the
east flushes out pale lavenders and pinks, then turns blood
red as it turns on itself, becoming a more definitive shape,
the more definitive, the bloodier. Until it sits, totally
unaware of the rest of the universe, waiting at the edge of a
sky that doesn't yet know what colors it wants to be, a hawk
waiting for the inevitable onset of human slaughter. The
light is fleeing.

Instead, sent a letter to feminist publisher in which said that she
composed her texts out of 'real' conversations, anything written
down, other texts, somewhat in the ways the Cubists had worked.
[Not quite true. But thought this statement understandable].
Cited, as example, her use of True Confessions stories. Such
stories whose content seemed purely and narrowly sexual,
composed simply for purposes of sexual titillation and economic
profit, if deconstructed, viewed in terms of context and genre,
became signs of political and social realities. So if the writer or
critic (deconstructionist) didn't work with the actual language of
these texts, the writer or critic wouldn't be able to uncover the
political and social realities involved. For instance, both genre
and the habitual nature of perception hide the violence of the
content of many newspaper stories.
    To uncover this violence is to run the risk of being accused of
loving violence or all kinds of pornography. (As if the writer

gives a damn about what anyone considers risks.)

Wrote, living art rather than dead has some connection with passion. Deconstructions of newspaper stories become the living art in a culture that demands that any artistic representation of life be non-violent and non-sexual, misrepresent.

To copy down, to appropriate, to deconstruct other texts is to break down those perceptual habits the culture doesn't want to be broken.

Deconstruction demands not so much plagiarism as breaking into the copyright law.

In the Harold Robbins text which had used, a rich white woman walks into a disco, picks up a black boy, has sex with him. In the Robbins text, this scene is soft-core porn, has as its purpose mild sexual titillation and pleasure.

[When Robbins' book had been published years ago, the writer's mother had said that Robbins had used Jacqueline Onassis as the model for the rich white woman.] Wrote, had made apparent that bit of politics while amplifying the pulp quality of the style in order to see what would happen when the underlying presuppositions or meanings of Robbins' writing became clear. Robbins as emblematic of a certain part of American culture. What happened was that the sterility of that part of American culture revealed itself. The real pornography. Clichés, especially sexual clichés, are always signs of power or political relationships.

BECAUSE SHE HAD JUST GOTTEN HER PERIOD, CAPITOL MADE A HUGE RED SATIN PILLOW CROSS THEN SMEARED HER BLOOD ALL OVER IT.

Her editor at the feminist publisher said that the Boss had found her explanation 'literary'. Later would be informed that this was a legal, not a literary, matter.

'HERE IT ALL STINKS,' CAPITOL THOUGHT. 'ART IS MAKING ACCORDING TO THE IMAGINATION. HERE, BUYING AND SELLING ARE THE RULES; THE RULES

OF COMMODITY HAVE DESTROYED THE IMAGINATION. HERE, THE ONLY
ART ALLOWED IS MADE BY POST-CAPITALIST RULES; ART ISN'T MADE
ACCORDING TO RULES.' ANGER MAKES YOU WANT TO SUICIDE.

Journalist who broke the 'Harold Robbins story' had been
phoning and leaving messages on writer's answer machine for
days. Had stopped answering her phone. By chance picked it up;
journalist asked her if anything to say.

'You mean about Harold Robbins?'

Silence.

'I've just given my publisher a statement. Perhaps you could
read that.'

'Do you have anything to add to it?' As if she was a criminal.

A few days later writer's agent over phone informed writer
what was happening simply horrible.

CAPITOL DIDN'T WANT TO MAKE ANY DOLLS.

How could the writer be plagiarizing Harold Robbins?

Writer didn't know.

Agent told writer if writer had phoned her immediately, agent
could have straightened out everything because she was good
friends with Harold Robbins' publisher. But now it was too late.

Writer asked agent if she could do anything.

Agent answered that she'd phone Harold Robbins' publisher
and that the worst that could happen is that she'd have to pay a
nominal quotation rights fee.

So a few days later was surprised when feminist publisher
informed her that if she didn't sign the apology to Harold
Robbins which they had written for her, feminist publishing
company would go down a drain because Harold Robbins or
Harold Robbins' publisher would slap a half-a-million [dollar?
pound?] lawsuit on the feminist publishing house.

Decided she had to take notice of this stupid affair, though her
whole life wanted to notice only writing and sex.

'WHAT IS IT?' CAPITOL WROTE, 'TO BE AN ARTIST? WHERE IS THE VALUE THAT
WILL KEEP THIS LIFE IN HELL GOING?'

For one of the first times in her life, was deeply scared. Was
usually as wild as they come. Doing everything if it felt good. So
when succumbed to fear, succumbed to reasonless, almost
bottomless fear.

Panicked only because she might be forced to apologize, not
to Harold Robbins, that didn't matter, but to anyone for her
writing, for what seemed to be her life. Book had already been
withdrawn from print. Wasn't that enough? Panicked, phoned her
agent without waiting for her agent to phone her.

Agent asked writer if she knew how she stood legally.

Writer replied that as far as knew Harold Robbins had made no
written charge. Feminist publisher sometime in beginning had
told her they had spoken to a solicitor who had said neither she
nor they 'had a leg to stand on'. Since didn't know with what she
was being charged, she didn't know what that meant.

Agent replied, 'Perhaps we should talk to a solicitor. Do you
know a solicitor?'

Knew the name of a tax solicitor.

Since had no money, asked her American publisher what to do,
if he knew a lawyer.

WOULD MAKE NO MORE DOLLS.

American publisher informed her couldn't ask anyone's advice
until she knew the charges against her, saw them in writing.

Asked the feminist publisher to send the charges against her
and whatever else was in writing to her.

Received two copies of the 'Harold Robbins' text she had
written twenty years ago, one copy of the apology she was
supposed to sign, and a letter from Harold Robbins' publisher to
the head of the feminist publishing company. Letter said that they
were not seeking damages beyond withdrawal of the book from

publication [which had already taken place] and the apology.

Didn't know of what she was guilty.

Later would receive a copy of the letter sent to her feminist publisher from the solicitor whom the feminist publisher and then her agent had consulted. Letter stated: According to the various documents and texts which the feminist publisher had supplied, the writer should apologize to Mr Harold Robbins. First, because in her text she has used a substantial number of Mr Robbins' words. Second, because she did not use any texts other than Mr Robbins' so there could be no literary theory or praxis responsible for her plagiarism. Third, because the contract between the writer and the feminist publisher states that the writer had not infringed upon any existing copyright.

When the writer wrote, not wrote back, to the solicitor that most of the novel in question had been appropriated from other texts, that most of these texts had been in the public domain, that the writers of texts not in public domain were either writers of True Confessions stories (anonymous) or writers who knew she had reworked their texts and felt honored, except for Mr Robbins, that she had never misrepresented nor hidden her usages of other texts, her methods of composition, that there was already a body of literary criticism on her and others' methods of appropriation, and furthermore, [this was to become the major point of contention], that she would not sign the apology because she could not since there was no assurance that all possible litigation and harassment would end with the signature of guilt, guilt which anyway she didn't feel: the solicitor did not reply.

Not knowing of what she was guilty, feeling isolated and pressured to finish her new novel, writer became paranoid. Would do anything to stop the pressure from the feminist publisher and simultaneously would never apologize for her work.

Considered her American publisher her father. Told her the 'Harold Robbins affair' was a joke, she should take her phone off the hook, go to Paris for a few days.

Finish your book. That's what's important.

WOULD MAKE NO MORE DOLLS.

Paris is a beautiful city.

In Paris decided that it's stupid to live in fear. Didn't yet know what to do about isolation. All that matters is work and work must be created in and can't be created in isolation. Remembered a conversation she had had with her feminist publisher. Still trying to explain, writer said, in order to deconstruct, the deconstructionist needs to use the actual other texts. Editor had said she understood. For instance, she was sure, Peter Carey in *Oscar and Lucinda* had used other people's writings in his dialogue, but would never admit it. This writer did what every other writer did, but she is the only one who admits it. 'It's not a matter of not being able to write,' the writer replied. 'It's a matter of a certain theory which is also a literary theory. Theory and belief.' Then shut up because knew that when you have to explain and explain, nothing is understood. Language is dead.

SINCE THERE WERE NO MORE DOLLS, CAPITOL STARTED WRITING LANGUAGE.

Decided that it's stupid living in fear of being forced to be guilty without knowing why you're guilty and, more important, it's stupid caring about what has nothing to do with art. It doesn't really matter whether or not you sign the fucking apology.

Over phone asked the American publisher whether or not it mattered to her past work whether or not signed the apology.

Answered that the sole matter was her work.

Thought alike.

Wanted to ensure that there was no more sloppiness in her work or life, that from now on all her actions served only her writing. Upon returning to England, consulted a friend who consulted a solicitor who was his friend about her case. This solicitor advised that since she wasn't guilty of plagiarism and since the law was unclear, grey, about whether or not she had breached Harold Robbins' copyright, it could be a legal precedent, he couldn't advise whether or not she should sign the apology. But must not sign unless, upon signing, received full and final settlement.

Informed her agent that would sign if and only if received full and final settlement upon signing.

Over phone, feminist publisher asked her who had told her about full and final settlement.

A literary solicitor.

Could they, the feminist publishing house, have his name and his statement in writing?

'This is my decision,' writer said. 'That's all you need to know.'

WROTE DOWN 'PRAY FOR US THE DEAD', THE FIRST LINE IN THE FIRST POEM BY CHARLES OLSON SHE HAD EVER READ WHEN SHE WAS A TEENAGER. ALL THE DOLLS WERE DEAD. DEAD HAIR. WHEN SHE LOOKED UP THIS POEM, ITS FIRST LINE WAS, 'WHAT DOES NOT CHANGE/ IS THE WILL TO CHANGE.'

WENT TO A NEARBY CEMETERY AND WITH STICK DOWN IN SAND WROTE THE WORDS 'PRAY FOR US THE DEAD.' THOUGHT, WHO IS DEAD? THE DEAD TREES? WHO IS DEAD? WE LIVE IN SERVICE OF THE SPIRIT. MADE MASS WITH TREES DEAD AND DIRT AND UNDERNEATH HUMANS AS DEAD OR LIVING AS ANY STONE OR WOOD.

I WON'T BURY MY DEAD DOLLS, THOUGHT. I'LL STEP ON THEM AND MASH THEM UP.

For two weeks didn't hear from either her agent or feminist publisher. Could return to finishing her novel.

Thought that threats had died.

In two weeks received a letter from her agent which read something like:

On your express instructions that your publisher communicate to you through me, your publisher has informed me that they have communicated to Harold Robbins your decision that you will sign the apology which his publisher drew up only if you have his assurance that there will be no further harassment or litigation. Because you have requested such assurance, predictably, Harold Robbins is now requiring damages to be paid.

Your publisher now intends to sign and publish the apology to Harold Robbins as soon as possible whether or not you sign it.

In view of what I have discovered about the nature of your various telephone communications to me, please contact me only in writing from now on.

Signature.

Understood that she had lost. Lost more than a struggle about the appropriation of four pages, about the definition of *appropriation*. Lost her belief that there can be art in this culture. Lost spirit. All humans have to die, but they don't have to fail. Fail in all that matters.

It turned out that the whole affair was nothing.

CAPITOL REALIZED THAT SHE HAD FORGOTTEN TO BURY THE WRITER DOLL. SINCE THE SMELL OF DEATH STUNK, RETURNED TO THE CEMETERY TO BURY HER. SHE KICKED OVER A ROCK AND THREW THE DOLL INTO THE HOLE WHICH THE ROCK HAD MADE. CHANTED, 'YOU'RE NOT SELLING ENOUGH BOOKS IN CALIFORNIA. YOU'D BETTER GO THERE IMMEDIATELY. TRY TO GET INTO READING IN ANY BENEFIT YOU CAN SO FIVE MORE BOOKS WILL BE SOLD. YOU HAVE BAGS UNDER YOUR EYES.'

CAPITOL THOUGHT, DEAD DOLL.

SINCE CAPITOL WAS A ROMANTIC, SHE BELIEVED DEATH IS PREFERABLE TO A DEAD LIFE, A LIFE NOT LIVED ACCORDING TO THE DICTATES OF THE SPIRIT.

SINCE SHE WAS THE ONE WHO HAD POWER IN THE DOLL-HUMAN RELATIONSHIP, HER DOLLS WERE ROMANTICS TOO.

Towards the end of paranoia, had told her story to a friend who was secretary to a famous writer.

Informed her that famous writer's first lawyer used to work

with Harold Robbins' present lawyer. First lawyer was friends with her American publisher.

Her American publisher asked the lawyer who was his friend to speak privately to Harold Robbins' lawyer.

Later the lawyer told the American publisher that Harold Robbins' lawyer advised to let the matter die quietly. This lawyer himself advised that under no circumstances should the writer sign anything.

It turned out that the whole affair was nothing.

Despite these lawyers' advice, Harold Robbins' publisher and the feminist publisher kept pressing the writer to sign the apology and eventually, as everything becomes nothing, she had to.

Knew that none of the above has anything to do with what matters, writing. Except for the failure of the spirit.

THEY'RE ALL DEAD, CAPITOL THOUGHT. THEIR DOLLS' FLESH IS NOW BECOMING PART OF THE DIRT.

CAPITOL THOUGHT, IS MATTER MOVING THROUGH FORMS DEAD OF ALIVE?

CAPITOL THOUGHT, THEY CAN'T KILL THE SPIRIT.

PATIENCE

AGNES OWENS

PATIENCE

The Castle

PATIENCE

It had been a long journey down — twenty-four hours it had taken. That's because we had come the cheapest way possible. First of all by train and boat, then train again and finally a tedious two hours by bus. The hotel room, which had been booked for us by the Continental Travel Agency, was small and cramped but otherwise clean. Somewhat dazed, I stared over the balcony outside the window. My sister Mary Jane squeezed in beside me at the rail. 'This isn't bad at all,' she said. 'What do you think?'

'Where's the sea?' I asked. Although the holiday brochure had said that the village was close to the Mediterranean, from where I stood we appeared to be in a valley — white cliffs on one side, rolling hills on the other and, facing us in the distance, a range of shadowy mountains.

'It can't be far away,' said Mary Jane, swivelling her head. 'Isn't that a castle on top of the cliff?'

'Where?' I asked, but now she was pointing down at the courtyard.

'Look at that fountain, all gushing with water! And those apartments over there by the river with their balconies and shutters. It's just how I imagined a French village would be — and all this lovely heat too. That's what I miss most about India — the heat.'

'It *is* warm,' I said, wiping my clammy forehead, 'But you'd have thought there would be more people about.' Down below the square was deserted apart from one old woman in dark clothes shuffling along the pavement with a bundle of sticks under her arm. 'Isn't this place supposed to be a popular tourist attraction?'

'The tourist season will be over by now. And I think it's perfect the way it is, slow moving and tranquil and all this sun. What more could one ask for?'

When I looked back at the small bedroom, barely big enough for one, I began to wish that we'd asked for separate rooms after all, but the booking had been done very much at the last minute, and it was probably too late now. And I supposed it was all very nice really, but being so hot and tired I wasn't in the mood to appreciate anything. Mary Jane suggested that after we'd had some lunch we could take a stroll along by the river, but all I wanted was to lie down. 'Actually I was thinking of having a rest afterwards,' I said.

'A rest?' she said incredulously. 'On the first day of our holiday?'

'But I'm tired. It would only be an hour at the most.'

'Honest to God, Dorothy — didn't you have enough sleep on the bus?' She went on to say that she hoped I wasn't going to spoil everything by being tired all the time for in that case I should have stayed at home. I thought that was a good one. She knew I hadn't wanted to come — but she'd harped on so much about it that I'd finally given in. 'We might never get another chance at our age,' she'd said at the time, mentioning father as an example of how easily one could go into a decline.

It never seemed to occur to Mary Jane to worry about money. Ever since she came home from abroad after father died — only for a visit, she said, but that was two years ago — she'd been spending it like water. Nor did it occur to her that half shares might be a bit unfair when I was the one who stayed home to take care of him while she went gallivanting all over the world 'having a wonderful time', as she said on her postcards. It was hard not to be bitter at times, but I tried to put the past out of my mind. There was the future to consider, after all. Now she was saying 'After all, you're only fifty-six — just two years older than me and look at you — fat as a pudding. It's exercise you need, not a rest.'

'I'll see how I feel later,' I said, thinking I'd rather be fat as a pudding than thin as a rake like her.

Lunch was served in the restaurant downstairs by the proprietor himself — a Monsieur Savlon whom we'd met briefly when we arrived. Weary though I was, I'd been struck by his singular appearance. He was almost as short as he was broad and without a single hair on his head. As if to make up for this his beard grew very thick and black. The meal he laid before us was heavy with sauce, and the predominant flavour was garlic, which I cannot stand. I left half of it on my plate and drank almost a jugful of water to get rid of the taste. When Monseiur Savlon came back to clear the table he asked me in perfectly good English, 'You do not like snails?' I shook my head and hurried off to the toilet where I was violently sick. Fifteen minutes later Mary Jane came up to the room and found me lying on top of the bed.

'You really are the limit,' she said. 'Don't you know snails are a delicacy?'

'I don't want to know anything,' I said, turning on my side and closing my eyes.

The next thing I knew she was towering above me in a long white cotton nightdress. 'What time is it?' I asked, for one horrible moment thinking it was father. For the last few years before he died he had worn a night-shirt that looked much the same.

'You may well ask,' she said, the freckles on her face standing out like half-pence pieces. 'You've been asleep for almost a day. I don't know how often I tried to wake you up but you simply refused. I was really fed up, I can tell you. And on top of that Monsieur Savlon kept asking about you. I didn't know what to say.'

'I'm sorry,' I said, forcing myself off the bed. I went out on to the balcony where the air was pleasantly cool. A mist hung over the river. The streets and the apartments looked fresh and sparkling. There was that air of quiet expectancy about the place you get first thing on a fine morning. I began to feel remarkably well.

'Let's go out as soon as we've had breakfast,' I suggested,' and see as much as we can before it gets too hot. We could even take a picnic to save us coming back for lunch. I'm sure Monsieur Savlon wouldn't mind.'

Mary Jane frowned. 'I hope you don't expect me to run around like a mad thing just because you've had a good rest. I haven't unpacked my things yet and I'll have to think about what to wear. I hate being rushed.'

I stifled a sigh. 'All right, we won't rush.'

In the restaurant Monsieur Savlon came over with a pot of coffee and a plate piled high with toast. 'You like?' he asked, his hands wavering over jars of honey, marmalade and jam. I nodded my head earnestly to wipe out any bad impressions I had given him previously.

'You want more?'

'No thanks,' said Mary Jane.

'This looks very appetising,' I said, and flushed, for no good reason I could think of.

'What a fussy little man he is,' said Mary Jane.

'He's only doing his best to please us,' I said, biting into a slice of toast and honey. When my plate was clean I asked her if she would mind telling him when she got the chance that I couldn't stand snails or garlic, but that this was no reflection on his excellent cooking.

'Tell him yourself,' she said.

'It doesn't matter,' I said, for I didn't want to admit that I sometimes feel shy with foreigners. I knew she would only jeer.

Mary Jane took a long time unpacking. Then she couldn't decide what to wear. 'Do you think I should put this on?' she said, holding up a dark blue dress which she had brought back from India, of a material so fine that it was almost transparent.

'Why not?' I said, 'It looks cool.'

She studied it, frowning. Then she shoved it back into the wardrobe. 'It's not casual enough for walking,' she complained. 'Anyone can see that.' Finally she settled for a pair of shorts and a T-shirt, saying that she might as well be comfortable. I thought that her thin white legs would have been better covered up, but there was no point in saying so, for she'd always go against anything I suggested. All the same, I began to feel overdressed in my skirt and blouse, so as a gesture of freedom I took off my tights. We were a few yards away from the hotel when I remembered that I'd forgotten to ask Monsieur Savlon for a picnic basket. I didn't mention this, however, for Mary Jane would have insisted on turning back and with the sun out in full force I was already too hot to be bothered. As we were passing the fountain Mary Jane brought a camera out of her bag and took a snapshot of water gushing from a lion's mouth into a basin floating with dead leaves.

'What's so special about that?' I asked.

'It will look splendid when it's enlarged and framed,' she said, looking at me pityingly. 'I do know what I'm talking about when it comes to photography, you know.'

When we were walking over the bridge Mary Jane stopped to take a shot of a woman on the other side of the road who was dragging a child along by the hand. When the woman began to shout angrily I hurried ahead. 'You shouldn't do that to people,' I said, when Mary Jane caught up with me. 'If you want to take photos of people we can take each other.' I turned down some steps which led on to the riverbank.

'It's characterization I want, not stodgy snaps of each other. Anyway, where are we going? I never said I wanted to go this way.'

'I thought you wanted to walk by the river.'

'I wanted to go to the castle,' she said huffily, shoving the camera back into her bag as if she had no further use for it, 'but it seems I've no choice.' When we reached a spot shaded by trees I said that I would have to sit down since my new sandals were rubbing.

'Oh no!' she groaned.

'But look,' I said, undoing the straps and showing her my heels, which were blistered and bleeding.

'You should have kept on your tights,' she said. 'What do we do now — go back?' She gave a hollow laugh and lay down on the grass with her hands behind her head. I could have wept with vexation at this point, but I knew it would be a mistake. Mary Jane has a cruel streak that thrives on my tears.

'What's wrong with staying here?' I said. 'It's cool and pleasant. At least we're outside.'

'I'm bored,' said Mary Jane. 'That's what's wrong. And anyway, you forgot to bring the picnic basket, didn't you?'

The lunch was good — cold salmon and salad. 'No garlic,' said Monsieur Savlon with a twinkle in his eye.

I wondered how he knew about the garlic. Perhaps Mary Jane had told him after all. She was in a good mood now, smiling broadly as she clutched her glass of wine. She had ordered a bottle, which I thought was far too much for so early in the day. By the time we had finished the meal more diners had arrived. I was glad for Monsieur Savlon's sake, because until now trade had been poor. After lunch Mary Jane offered to go into the village to buy some Elastoplast for my heels. I told her I'd be very grateful; at the same time I wondered how she was going to manage this, for she must have put away four or five glasses of wine by now.

As I watched her leave I noticed that she was walking very straight. Too straight, I thought. An hour later she came back and told me that she'd been wandering round the village and had seen some wonderful sights. There was one street in particular, she said enthusiastically, that had the most amazing houses — all different shapes and sizes with cute little courtyards filled with the most amazing flowers and plants. What a pity I hadn't been with her. Then she gave a large yawn and slumped into the chair.

'Did you remember the Elastoplast?' I asked.

'Goodness,' she said, 'I completely forgot.'

Dinner that evening was an excellent steak followed by a soufflé so light that it melted on the tongue. Mary Jane however, sat drowsily throughout the meal and eventually said she'd have to have an early night since the heat had completely worn her out. Much later I sat out on the balcony in the dark. There was nothing to see except the reflections of the bridge and the apartments cast upon the river by the street lamps. Behind me Mary Jane lay snoring. I looked at my watch. It was only half past nine.

The next morning when we were up and dressed Mary Jane said, 'Let's do something exciting. This is our third day and we've done nothing at all.'

'What do you suggest?'

'I was thinking about the castle.'

I pulled open the shutters. There was no cool morning mist — only the sun blinding my eyes. 'It's too hot for climbing,' I said.

'It won't get any cooler. This is the South of France, you know.'

'I'd never get up that cliff,' I protested.

'Don't be stupid. You don't go straight up the cliff. There's a path at the side. Monsieur Savlon told me.'

'Can't we leave it for another day? We've got plenty of time. We don't have to do everything all at once, surely?'

This threw her into a rage. 'We've done hardly anything,' she shouted. 'Honest to God, I wish I'd never come on this holiday. I can see it's going to be a right disaster.'

Suddenly I was infuriated by everything: the heat, this sombre village and most of all by Mary Jane. Things always had to go her way and that's what it had been like ever since she'd moved in. 'And I wish you'd never come to live with me in the first place,' I shouted back. Mary Jane's eyes narrowed and her mouth tightened ominously. I began to regret my words. I was afraid that she might start throwing things around the room and I didn't want Monsieur Savlon at the door.

'I'm sorry,' I said quickly. 'I didn't mean it. The words just slipped out.'

'You meant it, all right,' she said, storming out of the bedroom and banging the door behind her.

I followed her into the toilet and said that I was sorry, I'd spoken in a temper because I'd had a bad headache all morning, but if she was really set on going to the castle I would go with her. The main thing was for us not to fall out over trifles.

'Trifles?' she repeated, staring at me oddly in the mirror above the wash basin. 'So father was right about you after all.'

'What do you mean?' I demanded.

'As a matter of fact father wrote to me not long before he died, saying that you had terrible bouts of temper. He complained that you weren't the loving patient Dorothy he used to know. In fact, the poor thing even suspected that you were trying to poison him. He said he caught you putting something in his tea one night.'

'But he always drank cocoa,' I said, bemused.

'Anyway, by the time I arrived home he was already dead. So I decided it was best to let sleeping dogs lie, if you'll pardon the expression.'

I stared at her, outraged. Mary Jane would say anything to spite me, but to more or less accuse me of trying to poison father was going a bit far even for her.

'I gave him a tranquillizer every night to make him sleep. He died of a heart attack. It was on the certificate.'

'I don't doubt it was, but doctors can be careless.' She paused for a minute then added defensively: 'I'm only saying what he wrote.'

Mary Jane was an atrocious liar, I knew that. I wondered if there had ever been a letter at all. Before father died he had still been able to totter around, but I could hardly imagine him going out to buy a stamp. 'So if he thought I was poisoning him why didn't he cut me out of his will?'

Mary Jane gave a shrug. 'I'd never have mentioned it in the first place if you hadn't been so hurtful,' she said sulkily.

We were about to leave the hotel and head for the castle when Monsieur Savlon came running after us to tell us it was going to rain. Overhead the sky was as monotonously blue as ever. 'It can't,' said Mary Jane.

'It says on forecast it will rain.'

'Forecasts aren't always right,' Mary Jane snapped, and left him on the doorstep shaking his head.

We crossed the bridge and had just turned right into a narrow street which Mary Jane said should take us to the bottom of the cliff, when the sky darkened. A minute later it began to pour. In two seconds we were soaked through as we ran back to the café on the corner.

Men were playing cards round a table in the centre of the room, and behind the counter a very fat woman stood regarding us with a mixture of hostility and surprise. 'This doesn't look much like a café,' I said.

'I'll see what they've got,' said Mary Jane, going to the bar, while I dumped our bags on a table beside a window which was covered with wire mesh.

Mary Jane came back to the table with two glasses of milky looking stuff which according to her was all they sold, unless I preferred beer, of course.

'What is it?' I asked. 'Are you sure they don't have coffee?'

'Pernod,' she said. 'I told you they haven't.' She took a sip from the glass. 'It's not bad. Why don't you try it? It might take the miserable look off your face.'

'I'm not drinking that,' I said, feeling very agitated, because the card-players were staring across at us intently. When one of them winked and jerked his head over his shoulder as if to suggest that we join them I said to Mary Jane that we had better leave.

'Can't you take a joke?' Mary Jane began, but I was already on my feet and heading for the door with my bag in hand. Outside it was still raining but not so heavily. I made my way as fast as I could back to the hotel, and although I turned round once or twice to see if Mary Jane was following me, there was no sign of her.

Up in the room I took off my wet clothes and lay down under the bedcovers in my underslip, wondering whether to pack my bags straightaway or wait until tomorrow. The holiday was turning out much worse than I had anticipated and, if the past three days were anything to go by, there was no likelihood of it getting any better. In the end I gave up trying to work out what to do and fell asleep through sheer inertia.

'Madame, are you there?' Monsieur Savlon was shouting through the keyhole.

I sat up, startled. 'Yes. What is it?'

'Your sister is in the bar. I think she has too much to drink. She is lying on the floor.'

'I'll be down in a minute,' I called, but as soon as I heard his footsteps receding down the stairs I jumped out of bed and locked the door. As far as I was concerned Mary Jane could stay where she was. Right at this moment it was quite beyond me to cope with her.

Prompt on six o'clock I went into the restaurant, for the sandwiches in my bag were damp and soggy and I hadn't eaten since breakfast. There were a few other diners in the room but Mary Jane wasn't among them. I sat down at our usual table anticipating some sharp words from Monsieur Savlon; if he ordered us out it would solve the problem of whether to leave or not, but I dreaded having to face him all the same. However, he laid a bowl of soup in front of me and said quickly: 'Your sister she is sleeping in my mother's room. Do not worry. She will be fine.' Before I could thank him for his trouble he went on, 'Tonight I plan something special for you. I think you will like.' I looked up at him blankly. Hesitating, he added. 'Perhaps if Madame wears the nice dress she has on when she arrive it would be suitable for this plan.' Then without waiting for an answer, he disappeared into the kitchen.

Upstairs I searched for the dress he had mentioned and found it lying creased on the wardrobe floor. Anyway, what did it matter, I thought, since I wasn't going anywhere. If it was a surprise party he was talking about I didn't want any surprises. I would only feel awkward. I wouldn't be able to speak to anyone and I could envisage Mary Jane showing up drunk and making a spectacle of herself. I sat out on the balcony staring at the reflections on the river, wondering angrily if this was what I had come to France for. When I went back into the room, the wardrobe door was still open, and my eye fell on the dark blue dress that Mary Jane had brought back from India. I tried it on and it fitted me rather well. The cloth had been cut in such a way that it flared out under the high bodice, flattering my full figure. As I studied myself in the wardrobe mirror I decided that I'd never looked so elegant, and that I would go to this affair after all, if only to show my face.

There was no one in the bar except Monsieur Savlon and the tiny old woman who collected the tumblers from the tables on the terrace.

'Am I too early?' I asked. It was nine o'clock. I'd imagined everything would have been in full swing by now.

'No — no — you sit here,' said Monsieur Savlon, pointing to a table in the centre of the room. All the others had been stacked against the wall to clear a space on the floor. 'You will take some?' he said, opening a bottle of wine. 'Very good. Very old.' I sipped the wine, scarcely tasting it, as he sat down opposite me. 'I drink this only on my birthday,' he said.

'I see,' I said. 'You're having a birthday party?'

He frowned as if he did not quite understand. 'So I celebrate this with you.'

'How thoughtful,' I said faintly, as I caught the eye of the old woman who stood behind the bar counter watching us, nodding her head slightly as if in approval.

'You like music?' asked Monsieur Savlon.

'Yes. I do.'

'Then my mother will play.' He snapped his fingers at the counter, and as if a switch had been pressed the sound of violins filled the room. It struck me as all rather weird — the music, the absence of guests and in particular the fact that this small shabby woman was Monsieur Savlon's mother. I must say I would have expected someone more grand. 'You want to dance now?' he asked.

It was the last thing I wanted to do. I hadn't danced since my school days, when we had all been forced to take lessons, but I couldn't very well refuse him. As it happened Monsieur was an excellent dancer, which made it easy for me to follow his lead, and I began to enjoy myself exceedingly.

'The music is called "La Vie en Rose", he said, when he led me back to the table. Time passed quickly after that. We danced, then stopped to rest and sip our wine, savouring it slowly as befits a good one. After we had danced for about the sixth time — although I had lost count, really — Monsieur Savlon looked at his watch and said, 'We will now finish. It is late.' He called out to his mother, who had not moved an inch from her position behind the counter, and the violins played no more. I thanked Monsieur Savlon for a pleasant evening, but when I turned to thank his mother, she had gone, and it was with a pang of sadness that I climbed the stairs, for it seemed unlikely that such an evening would ever come my way again.

Mary Jane was sitting up in bed when I entered the room.

'Where the hell have you been?' she asked, in a voice sharp as tempered steel. 'And what are you doing with my dress on?' I explained that I had only been trying on the dress to see how it looked, and had forgotten to take it off when I went downstairs to the bar to look for her.

'You're lying,' she said. 'When I went down to the bar the door was locked. What's more, I could hear music.' I felt my face flushing as she squinted at me curiously. Then her eyes went wide with dawning realization. 'Don't tell me you were having it off with that old dwarf! My God, you must be desperate.'

Next morning Mary Jane told me that she was going to have another try at the castle. 'Do you want to come along?' she asked, pointing out that it wasn't as hot as before. 'I might as well,' I muttered, finding it difficult to look her in the face — particularly since at that very moment Monsieur Savlon put the coffee pot on the table with his usual brisk 'Good morning.' After he had gone Mary Jane leaned across the table and whispered. 'Mind you, he might not be such a bad catch when you think about it. Must be worth a mint.'

An hour later we were out in the middle of a field which had more stones than grass in it. Mary Jane was walking on ahead while I lagged behind, trying to keep a good distance between us.

'I've found the path,' she shouted 'Do hurry up.'

When I caught up with her she was sitting on a flat stone looking up at a rough track which led over baked earth and rock to the castle above. 'What do you think?' she asked. 'I think I'll manage,' I replied.

We began to climb. The path itself wasn't so terribly steep, but the effort of side-stepping over loose boulders tired me out. Mary Jane was always on ahead, but not by very much, and I was only minutes behind her when I reached the top.

'So you finally made it,' she said, as I stood there breathless, looking around for somewhere to rest my aching legs. 'There it is.' She pointed towards a heap of ruins at the edge of the cliff. She set off towards it, camera in hand, while I followed behind reluctantly. From close up, all that remained of the castle was a long narrow enclosure of stonework. Grass and flowers grew through the smashed flagstones, and the rampart wall on the edge of the cliff was broken in parts.

'That looks dangerous,' I said, but Mary Jane wasn't listening. She was too busy focusing the camera on the scene, aiming it this way and that, as if what she was doing was all so terribly important. I might have been amused at her antics if I hadn't been so busy watching where she put her feet.

'How about one of you,' she said, pointing the camera in my direction.

'Some other time. I'm not in the mood.'

'You never are in the mood,' she said. She gave an ugly laugh. 'Except if it's Monsieur Savlon, of course.'

'Don't start that again,' I said. I walked away from her and looked over the parapet wall. It was a sheer drop down to the river below. Mary Jane came to stand beside me. 'Magnificent, isn't it? You can see everything for miles around.'

I stepped back. My head was beginning to spin. 'I must have a drink of water,' I said, turning back into the enclosure.

We sat on two flat stones and drank from our flasks without looking at each other. 'I've been thinking things over,' Mary Jane said, 'and I might as well tell you I've decided to go back to India. I had a letter from Lady Bonham Fletcher and apparently she misses me terribly and is desperate to have me back. I wasn't going to go, because I didn't want to leave you on your own, but the way things are going . . .' She let her voice tail off, as if there was no need for further explanation.

'Why don't you?' I said. Knowing what a liar she was, I was positive she had no intention of going to India. 'I'm sure it's the best thing you could do.'

'So we'll have to sell the house,' she added.

'What do you mean — sell the house?'

'It's plain enough. I'm entitled to half of father's estate and if I'm leaving the country, the only way I can get it is for us to sell the house.'

'Mary Jane,' I said. 'Please stop all this nonsense. I know you don't mean a word of it.'

'Oh but I do,' she broke in. 'I want the house sold. It's as simple as that. And anyway' she went on, 'you've got to admit it's in a terrible state — all that old piping and the place is rotten with damp. Just think, with your share you could buy yourself a nice little flat. It would be so much cheaper to run and easier to clean.'

My throat had gone dry. I began to trace circles in the dust with my finger. Mary Jane stared at me stonily. 'Aren't you going to say anything? You've got to face facts, you know. You've really no option.'

'Perhaps you're right,' I said at last, 'I might be better off in a small flat. I can't say I'd considered it before, but if you say you're going back to India . . .'

'Of course I'm right,' she said with such obvious relief that I didn't know whether to laugh or cry. 'Well now,' she went on cheerfully. 'I must take a photo of you in front of the castle. Something to look back on.'

It turned out that there was too much shade there for the camera, and Mary Jane moved me on. 'I'll take it over by the wall,' she said. 'It's brighter there.' After a bit of manoeuvering to get the exact focus she clicked the shutter. 'That's it,' she said. 'Now you can take one of me.'

'By the wall?'

'Of course, by the wall.'

Mary Jane took up a pose with one arm arranged on top of the wall. 'Move over a bit,' I said, 'You're too far to the left.'

'For goodness sake,' she said irritably. Fixing her smile on the camera, she took a step sideways. Then her arm flailed in empty space and she went backwards through the gap without uttering a word of protest.

Mary Jane was buried in the village cemetery. The coroner's verdict was accidental death. Monsieur Savlon came to the funeral along with a few of the old village women, including his mother. It was a simple affair. The coffin was placed inside a marble tombstone and a priest said a few brief words. As I was leaving the cemetery Monsieur Savlon came up to offer his condolences. 'Be patient, Madame,' he said, 'Time will heal your pain.'

Personally I thought I'd been patient long enough. Through my tears I told him that it would have been some consolation to visit my sister's grave at least once a week, but alas, I couldn't even do that. Monsieur Savlon stopped and confronted me. 'But why not? You can stay for as long as you want — forever, if you wish.'

'Forever?' I said, with astonishment.

'Forgive me,' he said. 'I have offended you perhaps. It is not the right time to say this.'

'I'll think about it,' I said, turning away and wiping my eyes.

I am taking up Monsieur Savlon's offer. It's the best thing that could have happened. He has told me that there's an apartment across the river which is empty. He knows the owner very well and he's sure that if he enquires for me I'll get it. He assures me that the rent won't be too dear, since it's a poor village and no one is expected to pay more than they can afford. I can scarcely get over my good luck. After all those years of stagnating in father's old house I'm about to live in an apartment in a French village with a balcony overlooking the river. Of course I'm sad about Mary Jane, in a way. But she was her own worst enemy. Which reminds me — I must get rid of her writing bureau before I sell the house. That's where she kept all her correspondence under lock and key, and as she said herself, it's better to let sleeping dogs lie. I still can't help feeling angry, though, when I think of her calling Monsieur Savlon a dwarf. How dare she say that about such a nice little man.

JUSTICE

SARA MAITLAND

JUSTICE

An Allegory

JUSTICE

Justice was born on Independence Day.

When her mother, Neme, dancing to the victory drums with her two thousand sisters of the National Women's Corps in the great central square of the new capital, felt the first tremors of her labour pains, she laughed and planned to call her child Freedom. But when she left the square and the blazing triumphant fireworks to go to the women's clinic down the hill, she discovered that, despite promises, there was no supply of the drug that her baby's eyes would need to counteract Neme's syphilis — contracted at the same moment as her child was conceived — she changed her mind and called the little girl Justice instead.

So Justice was born blind, on Independence Day, just before midnight, with the light of a thousand bonfires and two thousand fireworks shining down on her fierce, damp, little head, although she would never see them.

Neme had been an officer in the National Women's Corps. They were swift and deadly and strong. They ran all night chanting the songs of freedom, fifty miles a night to kill in the morning, and as they ran they breathed together, so perfectly in step that the velvet black air of the veldt drummed with their running. Even the men of the freedom army were afraid of them and they knew it and it made them feel powerful.

Neme had been with the Women's Corps when they had run all night to the small village where the Children's Camp was and there she had seen three hundred and eighty-two babies of the revolution being shelled to death, there she had seen seven- and eight-year-old children arm themselves with kitchen knives against the coming assault. Just before sundown, despite a courageous struggle the village defences had fallen and the well-armed, well-fed, fat soldiers of the enemy poured over the river and burned and stabbed and raped and looted.

The stories they told afterwards all said that no one who had been at the defence of that village, renamed after Independence the Village of Lamentation, was ever quite the same again.

Nonetheless victory finally came. From all three of the Friendly Borders, and from the hollows of the rock deep inside their homelands, the triumphant Freedom Army poured out and began its long march to the capital. Through villages of song and isolated farmsteads of flowers the Women's Corps had run, cheering and laughing. Neither pregnancy nor syphilis had deterred Neme from running with them and just nine months after the fall of the Village of Lamentation she was dancing to the victory drums with her two thousand sisters of the National Women's Corps in the great central square of the new capital for the Independence Day celebrations.

But after Independence Day there came a difficult time for Neme. Men had been frightened of the Women's Corps and did not like to remember that. Dreams were shattered now by the memory of the black night drumming to the two thousand feetfall of the Women's Corps passing. Those that had stayed in their beds and slept through those velvet nights were ashamed. Those who had daughters looked at these women and looked at their cookpots: two thousand women who knew how to fight better than they knew how to cook. It was alarming. Those who had been with their Leader to the Ice City, those who returned after years of exile in pale cold countries; they all felt that women should not be like these women, that it was not a credit to the Nation. A civilized Nation took care of its women.

The women were Heroes of the Nation.

The women were redundant heroes.

They were offered rehabilitation, which meant secretarial training, but it did not suit many of them, and afterwards there were no jobs. 'There are no jobs,' Neme thought, 'for a woman trained in the handling of high explosives, who has commanded others to kill, who has killed herself, who has a disease and a blind child.' Some of the women who were not rehabilitable, along with some of the men who seemed to have no talent for peace, were given land grants along the Unfriendly Border: a plan half dismissive and half defensive. Before Justice was a year old Neme took her from the capital out to the edge of the desert and tried to settle down on her farm there, tried to return to the village life of her childhood.

But she could not forget the bemused look in her brother's eyes as the six bullets had gone into his stomach.

But she could not forget the tiny foot, paler in the soft unformed arch, redder at the severed ankle, that she had found in her hand during the assault on the Village of Lamentation.

But she could not forget the eight hands that had held her down in turns while she was raped after the fall of the Village of Lamentation.

But she could not forget the fear in the men's eyes when the Women's Corps had formed up in the evenings. Fear, not pride. Fear, not love.

Neme turned to the darkness, to broodings of revenge and punishment. The songs of freedom turned in her mouth to prophecies of doom. She became one of the Furies and ran out at night across the veldt, now drumming with the power of her anger and her loneliness. She had long night talks with the Spirits of the Ancestors, who encouraged her towards vengeance and spite. Her chickens were unfed, her crops unhoed. Farming was not a subject that interested her. Her daughter was unfed, her hair uncombed. Justice was not a subject that interested her.

Yet Justice grew. More or less. Skimpy, ungenerously drawn against so huge an atmosphere, stripped down to the bone by neglect and by the harsh sand carried over the border by the unfriendly wind, grains of peril and alarm, sharpened by habits of hatred too many centuries old. Eyes enormous black pits, stretched from the strain of seeing nothing. Ears huge as night bats' crinkled from the strain of hearing everything. She grew like a root in dry land, with no charm or loveliness, no beauty, despised and rejected. A child of sorrows acquainted with grief, but fierce with her eager need to survive, honed on hunger and anger. Frail, tough, enduring, a child destined for the rise and fall of many in that land and beyond its borders.

And when she had passed through puberty she finally turned her back on the desert, the harsh wind, and her mother. She could not have explained why she went or what she was seeking, unlike her mother Neme, who at the same age had watched a white policeman shoot her brother dead on a back street and had slipped away from her own home to seek the hidden liberation army. Justice did not have that clarity, but her anger was huge and boiling, roaring inside her, disturbing her peace, making it impossible for her to hear the contours and shapes of the real things around her. She knew she could not stay down in the wilderness for ever. Something out there was calling her, and it was a call she could not resist. Without question she set out and groped her way back along the road towards the new capital.

For a week she sniffed and fondled her way along the road, her ears flapping delicately, swivelling like radar dishes to catch the whisper of her route, attuned to the distant soundings of her summons, like a whale in the great tidal currents hearing the song of its beloved seven oceans away. And on the first day of the new week, early, while it was still dark, Justice stumbled into the compound of the Mission of Our Lady of the Seven Sorrows where Mercy Cameron had just arrived to work as a volunteer for two years.

Mercy was born on Christmas Eve.

When her mother, Patience, humming to the echoes of the choir boys rehearsing their carols in the Cathedral, felt the first tremors of her labour pains, she laughed and planned to call her child Holly. But by the time she had rung her friend and midwife, organized someone to take care of her toddler, promised her oldest daughter a new baby for Christmas, located her busy husband and climbed the stairs to her own bedroom she realized that the baby was eager to be born. It was her fourth labour and was to prove the easiest of all six: by the time the midwife arrived Patience was sitting up, smiling, her new daughter still attached to its umbilical cord lying suckling on her breast.

'Well, that's a mercy,' said Patience's husband with a smile, thinking of the long night's work that faced him and the exhausting joy of a cathedral Christmas for a Canon with four small children. So they called the baby Mercy.

Mercy was born on Christmas Eve, just before midnight, with the light of a hundred Christmas tree bulbs and two hundred mellow gold candles lit for the midnight mass shining down on her golden, damp, little head. And before she and her mother curled down together for their first night's sleep she had been adored by her big sisters, blessed by a bishop, kissed by her mother's best friend. And amid a cascade of ancient bells her father, comfortable in his rôle, happily weary and grinning with almost boyish delight, had carried the white wafer, the sacred host, that cradled in its inmost essence the new-born Christ child to the bedside of his wife. And thus their newest daughter was made welcome in the world.

She was born in an ancient cobbled close, with velvet green lawns under the shadow of a great spire which rose with a breathtaking élan, both pointing and floating over the whole small city. Throughout her childhood the deep bells and the subtle gradations of colour in the creamy stones around her from bright dawn to soft dusk sang in gentle murmurs to the child.

Patience was a woman of the daylight. She had that deep natural courtesy that only women who have never had to know real anxiety can develop. Her dreams, her ancestors, all taught her of certainty and gentleness and kindness and generosity. She loved her husband, who was worthy of her love. She loved her house and the cathedral and the religion that nourished her and her family. She loved all her six children with a calm passion that was good for them; but, perhaps because of the ease of her labour, perhaps because of the deep joy for her of sharing the birth of her own child with Mary — her mother and friend, she always had a special warmth for Mercy. The sort of tenderness which occurs sometimes in large families from which none of the other children are the losers, but which is a cause of happy mirth and family jokes.

And Mercy grew. Simply and easily. She was a golden chubby baby and might have been spoiled by too much petting, had not her attentive parents noticed in her a deep sturdy intelligence, which they nurtured generously and with pride. What child could fail to thrive in so welcoming an atmosphere, so wrapped in love and companionship and joy, so nourished by the length of history in the town and the depth of greenness in the countryside around her, and with so much affectionate wisdom and care from parents whose natural benignity had been mellowed further by habits of love and security so many centuries old?

She grew like a tree standing by the water, loving and beloved. She was surrounded by every privilege, even the rare privilege of knowing that the privileged must serve in order to enjoy. So when she had finished her university degree she volunteered herself to benign relief charity and flew away from the gentle quadrangles of her home to teach for two years at the Mission of Our Lady of the Seven Sorrows.

So now Justice and Mercy have met; righteousness and peace have kissed one another.

Despite its rather gloomy name, the Mission of Our Lady of the Seven Sorrows was a joyful place. The Sisters of the Rose of Sharon, an obscure missionary teaching order, had arrived in that small valley before the turn of this century, and not being a patronized or prosperous community had not built in brick and mortar, let alone stone sent from half a world away. Their small chapel, convent and school were all hand-built in local wood and painted white, with wide verandas and neatly brushed paths. More recently the order had been more successful than many in its indigenization programme and more than half the white wimples framed black faces and their work was more useful because of it. The Sisters worked hard, sang their daily office to the accompaniment of local flutes and drums, and dug deep roots, and worked for their community. They adored Mercy, half hoped she would stay with them forever and knew she would not. They welcomed Justice from the road, fed her, bathed her, and watched the growing love between the two young women with delighted affection.

For indeed it was a love to delight in, and grew like a green bay tree. The wilderness and the dry land were glad for Justice and Mercy; at the labour of their hands and hearts the desert rejoiced and blossomed, blossomed abundantly like a rose and rejoiced with joy and singing. The glory of Lebanon was given to their love, the majesty of Carmel and Sharon. For a love so strong and free would open the eyes of the blind and unstop the ears of the deaf; the lame would leap like deer and the tongues of the dumb sing for joy. For waters broke forth in the wilderness and streams in the desert; the burning sand became a pool and the thirsty ground springs of water.

For two years they lived and loved and worked together, growing all the time in wisdom and knowledge. Mercy saw into Justice's deep fierce heart and recognized the iron, the ruthless unbending core of her friend and although she was awestruck she was not afraid. Justice saw into Mercy's warm soft heart and recognized the clear deep pool of her friend's truth and although she was touched she was not contemptuous. And Mercy found the hard, skinny roughness of Justice's body very beautiful and pleasing to her. And Justice found the soft rich smoothness of Mercy's body very beautiful and pleasing to her.

And they worked. Each day they rose at dawn and went out while it was still cool to dig the well that was to change the lives of the women around them. They dug themselves, till their hands were cracked and the dust in their furrows could not be scrubbed clean. They inspired others to work. Justice argued fiercely, sounding like Neme in her young days, to persuade the men to dig with their women. Mercy wrote long humble letters to her father and his friends to raise money to pay for the well-shaft lining. When the hole got deeper and deeper and still there was no water they had to work to keep faith and hope and courage alive. Justice's throat was weary from chanting the songs of struggle and Mercy's eyes were glazed from the sun and the stubbornness of her own will. Then one morning there was water in the hole. And despite the gloomy predictions of the village patriarchs, the water gushed up, pure and clean, and kept on flowing. The women of the village stood nervous and shy, their babies on their hips, unable to believe what they were seeing. Then Justice and Mercy lowered buckets down the hole and threw water at each other, poured it over the heads of the smaller children who were frightened at first, watching this most precious and laborious substance being wasted; and then when they saw that the well was filling up and overflowing, that the water sparkled in the morning sunshine like diamonds, the children giggled and splashed and dabbed at the water with their toes, until everyone came to play with them.

Suddenly all the village was laughing and singing. They held a great party. The Sisters of the Rose of Sharon hitched up their white habits, paddled in the mud that flooded the village and sang

Behold I saw water proceeding from the right side thereof,
And all to whom the water came, they cried Alleluia.

They worked. Each morning after the heat became too great for digging, Mercy held her classes on the wide cool veranda of the Mission House and taught the children and their parents to read. And Justice sat on the dry earth under the shade of the maniveri trees and taught the parents and their children the drumming songs of freedom and told them the brave stories of the ancestors, and of the National Women's Corps, who had run all night and fought all day so that they could own their own well and their own fields and their own history.

They worked. After the lessons were over and the students all gone home, Mercy stood with the Sisters, pink and golden beside their white and black, and dispensed medicine and advice and food in the clinic, and held the hands of mothers who were scared for their babies, and children who were fearful for their mothers. And Justice, her ears attuned to the solidness and ripeness of fruit, to the sprouting of weeds, to the underground mutterings of peanuts and to the tidiness of the white maize rows, bowed her back and hoed and weeded and picked and gathered so that there was food for them all to eat.

And when the sun had gone down they would sit, close together, skin to skin, leaning against the wooden walls and listen while the Sisters sung compline to the accompaniment of the local pipes, and their two bodies would melt together so that without Mercy there was no Justice and without Justice there was no Mercy and they were contented.

Eventually it was time for Mercy to go home. She had joyfully stayed far longer than the two years which she had initially undertaken, and she could have stayed on even longer. But her mother's letters sounded bravely plaintive and her heart was touched. She urged Justice to come with her. At first Justice argued that they should stay where they were, where they were needed, where they were happy. Mercy begged her. She thought about her mother and was a little homesick; she missed books and classical music and northern stars and the gentler sunshine of her home; she hoped that perhaps in that more technically advanced country they might be able to cure Justice's eyes, to give her back her sight. If not, then Justice could at least learn to read braille, learn the hundred skills that the poverty of the new country could not afford to give her, and then they would be able to do more work, and more usefully. Then, later perhaps, they could both come back together with new and greater skills, and live there for ever.

Justice was uncertain. Perhaps Mercy should go home without her for a visit and then she would return because Justice would hold the reins of her heart and tug them gently to guide Mercy back across the oceans.

It made good sense, but in the meantime neither of them could bear the thought of being without her friend.

Justice went for a long walk to try and work it out. For three days she walked through heat and night. She listened to the shadow of the noon-day, her skin prickled from the touch of starlight, she smelled the deep dryness of the world and asked the earth beneath her feet what it desired. And then from far away she felt both the excitement and the fear that was in her to travel and see the uttermost reaches of the world. She could not bear the thought of being defeated by fear, she could not bear the thought of being without her beloved. Mercy had been in her country for all these years and it was only fair that she should go to Mercy's, at least for a little while.

After three days walking she returned, thin and fierce as ever and agreed with Mercy that they should leave.

So they kissed the Sisters farewell, and turned their faces to the north. Each day as they travelled the honey-coloured stars of the Southern Cross lay closer and closer to the horizon until one day they could not see them at all. And each day after that the pole star, diamond and glittering rose higher in the sky and twinkled at them. Each day as they travelled it got colder and colder and Justice had to wear more and more clothes which she did not find comfortable and which made her look plainer than ever to all eyes except Mercy's. The sharp sparkles of cold grated on Justice's delicate ears; the smell of the frost drowned out the cryptic scented messages by which she usually found her pathway. She felt lost and frightened.

It was not just the cold. Justice found all the sounds and the smells of the northlands oppressive and difficult at first. When she swivelled her radar ears to catch the music of her adventurous calling a thousand other sounds crashed in; when she raised her delicate nose to find her way it was blasted by ghastly scents, overwhelmed by malodorousness. At first then she became quiet and orderly, delicate and timid like a wild animal, ready to start away and yet hampered and confined by her blindness as she had not ever been before. People admired Mercy for rescuing Justice, congratulated her on her goodness and nobility. This confused Justice altogether and she responded with an unexpected gratitude and humility. But inside her the roaring, which had been subdued by happiness and business at the Mission of Our Lady of the Seven Sorrows began to crescendo again, building up inside her, drowning the sounds outside.

As soon as they had landed in Mercy's home country, Mercy went to visit Patience. Justice, of course, went with her. Mercy's parents were glad to have their lovely sweet daughter safe home again and they made Justice welcome for her sake. They were proud of their daughter for her kindness and generosity to the sweet little oppressed child they thought they saw in front of them. They gave good advice and recommended doctors, specialists, who had been at the university with Mercy's father and would, they were sure, on a letter of reference from them, do all they could for Justice's eyes and her suitable training. For all their years of wisdom and goodness they had no experience by which to gauge the wild fierceness which was at the heart of Justice. Content with each other and protected from the rest of the world by their faith and by their comfort they had no way of recognizing the power and splendour of the love that the two younger women had for each other. It did not occur to Justice to explain something that was so obvious to her; and Mercy, recognizing for the first time that there were limits to her parents' openness, struggled to understand their difficulty. Kindly and gently she decided that it would be kinder to say nothing.

Nonetheless the visit was wrapped in a warm tranquillity. Although it was shallow, it was happy and comfortable for all of them. Patience sat quietly in her sunfilled sitting room, the roses in her garden blooming again more gently in the faded chintz covers to her armchairs. The room was peaceful: a low hum of cut flowers and lemon furniture polish on old mahogany were the only sounds inside; the grass growing in the close and the sunshine falling on the cobbles were the only sounds outside, except when the great bells rang. Justice loved the quiet because within it she could at last hear her space again; although it smelled entirely different, she thought the room sounded very like the Mission of Our Lady of the Seven Sorrows. But even more than she loved the quiet she loved the bells; their deep complicated interweavings of sound made an orderly shape to the roaring inside her; they filled her emptiness and gave her a new peace that she had never known before. In this peace her fierceness returned to her, and suddenly she was greedy for struggle and victory. She accepted the peace and the greed and the fierceness as a gift from Patience and told Mercy that she loved Patience and that it was time for them both to move on.

Mercy was glad that Justice loved her mother, but when she put her arms around Justice she felt her fierceness. Mercy could sense at once the drum beat of tension and excitement and then she was more than glad, she was exultant, she rejoiced in the joy of her friend. She knew it was time for them both to move on.

Patience could sense the joy and energy for her daughter and knew with generosity that it was time for the two girls to move on. One afternoon she took a quiet opportunity to set them free. Her hands rested peacefully on her *petit point* and her concentration rested peacefully on her daughter. She said,

'Well, darling, what are you going to do now?'

'Work for Justice,' said Mercy.

Her mother smiled at the enthusiasm and idealism of this her favourite child.

'You can't change the world overnight, you know. But good luck.'

Both Mercy and Justice received Patience's blessing with

pleasure and set off for the northern capital, the cruel Ice City.

Ah. The chilly streets, the icy corners, the frozen depths, the frost-bound beauty of the Ice City. The buildings of glass and steel so tall and dazzling that a person walked between them as in a glacial crevasse. The sun, small and white and far away, refracted glitter off the shiny cliffs but warmed nothing. The cold bounced from brilliant planed surfaces and the light was always blue with the frost of centuries. Deep underground the people like mice ran down the cold tunnels seeking for their lives and not finding them. From each sharp corner icicles, honed by centuries into pointed stalactites, hung poised to crash through the skull and into the brain of anyone who spoke too loudly, too demandingly, who shouted on the street corners of warmth and equality and passion and kindliness; and in every frozen puddle tiny, trapped rainbows born of oil and shimmering neon struggled to escape their prisons.

Justice was blind and could not see the menacing icicles.

Justice could smell the stink of corruption that the frost covered over for those whose noses were less sensitive.

Justice could hear the whine of fear that the tinkling and sparkling of the ice overlaid for those whose ears were less well attuned.

Justice could feel the hearts of loneliness that thick woollen gloves smoothed out for those whose finger tips were less practised.

Justice was so blind so she could not understand the difference between black and white.

Justice was in love with Mercy so she could not understand the difference between male and female.

Justice came from a country made poor by this land's richness so she could not understand the difference here between rich and poor.

Justice knew only about good and evil. She loved the first because it sounded and smelled and felt and tasted like Mercy and like the gentle Sisters at the Mission of Our Lady of the Seven Sorrows. She hated the second because it fought against the first and blotted out the sharp edges of her clarity.

Justice stood up on the street corners and sang her judgement on the Ice City:

> I will show strength with my arm,
> I will scatter the proud in the imagination of their hearts;
> I will put down the mighty from their seats;
> I will exalt the lowly.
> I will fill the hungry with good things,
> And send the fat cats away empty.
> I am going to set at liberty those who are oppressed
> And proclaim the acceptable year of Jubilees.

Mercy was appalled. 'But Justice,' she said plaintively, 'Who then shall be saved?'

'Only they who have clean hands and pure hearts, who have not lifted up their lips unto falsehoods, nor sworn so as to deceive their neighbours.'

'Oh Justice,' said Mercy lovingly, 'You don't understand.'

'Look around you, Mercy,' said Justice ferociously, 'Look what's happening here. Oppression, rape, frostbite, ignorance, capitalism, colonialism, sexism, racism, and all the little children ... I don't want to understand, I want it to stop.'

'But you have to understand. About psychology and the passing on of oppression and inheritance and history and simple stupidity.'

'No,' said Justice.

'Yes,' said Mercy, 'Yes, to understand all is to forgive all.'

So they went to work.

'What we need here,' said Justice, 'is a different branch of the Mission of Our Lady of the Seven Sorrows. In my warm country it was right to console the sufferers of sorrows, but here in this cold country I think we should inflict sorrows.'

'Couldn't we do both?' asked Mercy.

'That seems fair enough,' said Justice.

So they did.

Justice went through the Ice City, sniff, sniff, sniff, like a hound, and when she smelt out injustice, corruption and abuse she quivered like a pointer, standing stiff, her fingers pointing out in front of her and her ears lifting forward, ready like a guard-dog to move in for the kill. She did not discriminate: all injustice was injustice to her — the rich industrialist who exploited his labour force, the poor man who beat his wife, the thief who stole five pence and the robber-baron who stole millions. She would not listen to market forces when she smelled out usury; and she would not listen to deprivation when she sniffed out thuggery. Justice judged, but she did not punish. She moved calmly through the Ice City requiring of the unjust repentance, reparation and restitution.

Mercy walked beside her, giving to the judged compassion, cuddles and caring. Mercy could always find a reason, and the reason explained everything to her and she did not find forgiveness difficult. Her deep love for the sinner swallowed up the sin and replaced it with pardon, with generosity, with love.

As they went on their way Justice was usually silent but Mercy was usually singing. She sang rich strong songs and their rhythms were the ancient sturdy ones of buried and silenced histories, of work done necessarily and lovingly a thousand ages ago or yesterday; the songs that mothers sing to their babies on their breasts, the songs that are marched to by those who march out freely to fight without weapons for their own truths. They were songs that returned to people their pasts and so gave them new presents and future hopes.

The two women were always side by side and because they so loved each other and trusted each other, because each night they met again and embraced and re-learned the contours of each other's flesh, because there was no rivalry and no separation between them, because there was nothing but joy and love between, then they were happy and useful.

Some mornings when the sun was shining, and Justice was sniffing and Mercy was singing, a new thing could be seen in the Ice City — the odd drip of something liquid, of water, or at least the dream of water, would quiver for a moment on the end of an icicle, would splash, plop, plop, plop, onto the rigid pavements, and some child seeing this lovely round globule, hearing the funny splashy plop noise, would laugh, covering its face with its hands as though ashamed, but still the gleeful giggle would break out.

Sometimes at midday those who still knew how to raise their eyes and look around them would think, questioningly to themselves, 'perhaps . . . well . . . Does the sun perhaps look a bit different to-day, a little yellower maybe, or a little nearer?' And that slight, almost imaginary, change in the sun would remind old men of Mercy's songs, would remind old women of their childhood when there were more colours, greens and golds and blues. Some even noticed that the yellower sun was a warmer sun, and risked pulling back the cuff of a mitten and letting those frail shafts of gold touch their skin.

One evening some of the more active and observant citizens even noticed that high high up the icy glass cliffs there were faint glimmers, faint reflected hints of a colour which would have to be called pink — rose pink, someone suggested, stumbling over the words.

Justice and Mercy reached out their hands, unspeaking, almost shy with excitement, and touched each other very gently. They grinned, they laughed, they whooped uproariously down the street while icicles fell into soggy little mountains of mush beside them. They laughed and danced in the streets and then they went out to recruit more members of their National Women's Corps, of the Sisterhood of the Seven Sorrows.

And then one day Mercy did a very foolish thing. A thing that only a woman would be foolish enough to do and only a man would be stupid enough to misunderstand and take advantage of.

The two of them went hunting down one of the deepest and darkest of the tunnels of the Ice City. And they came to a murky corner where no hint even of the coldest sun had ever come. And there Justice sniffed out a man who had been cruel, who had beaten his wife and abused his daughter. Justice pronounced judgement on him, with all her power, and she was in full strength that day. The contempt and anger that she felt for him cut through all the layers of clothing in which he wrapped himself and laid him naked and humiliated in front of the crowd who gathered. Then that was not enough and she flayed him, stripped his skin off him, proclaiming his shame and wickedness to all the world. He heard her judgement and was baffled. He did not understand why what he had done was so wicked that Justice would stand over him and speak such harsh words. He felt that the great holes where her eyes should have been failed to detect that he was beautiful and spoiled; failed to acknowledge that his wife was a shrew and that her children hampered him and limited him; failed to acknowledge that his daughter had enjoyed it, had begged him for fun and seduced him for her own pleasure; and failed to understand that there was never quiet in his house and none of them held him in proper respect. He had not meant to hurt them, of course, but they were his women, and it was none of Justice's business, and that was just the sort of a man that he was. It was not, any of it, his fault.

Mercy saw the confusion in his face and put her arms around him, gently and lovingly, like his mother. She rocked him in her arms and offered him forgiveness. He was beautiful, almost as beautiful as he thought he was, and he was sad, and he was confused. Mercy was moved. She left Justice and led the poor sad confused man home through the streets. And because he put his arms round her so trustfully, and because he seemed so sad and confused and childlike, she did not only give him her com-passion and her understanding, she exonerated him. She said,

'It doesn't matter. It doesn't matter.'

They were the words she had never said before. Because she told him that it did not matter, and because she was kind and gentle and soft just as he thought a real woman should be, when she refused his less tender, more demanding embraces he was very angry. When she tried to explain that she refused him not because there was anything wrong with loving desire, but because she loved Justice with all the love she had available, he was furious.

He raped her and he beat her, just so that she would shut up and acknowledge that he was a man and it was her duty to obey him. But she could not do that. So he left her battered and bloody.

When Justice found her she was dying.

'How could you do this?' Justice asked sternly, standing over her dying friend.

Mercy whimpered, 'You don't understand.'

'I never wanted to,' said Justice. 'I'm going to tell you one last thing, Mercy my sweet friend. To understand all is to forgive all and to change precisely nothing.'

And although she wept acidic tears which burned deep crevasses into the rough skin of her face, she would not hold Mercy's hand when she died.

Justice without Mercy was like a rat in the sewers of the Ice City. She gnawed at the lies that formed its foundations, till they crumbled and there was no place of comfort. No Charlotte Corday with a carving knife was ever so present in the bathrooms of the citizens as Justice was.

Justice went beyond judgement now. Justice dealt out retribution and reward, undistracted by seeing, by loving, by touching. Justice handled the executions swiftly and without compunction.

The City ruled by Justice was colder than ever, colder than it had been before she came. The faint whispers of colour and moisture that had begun to return were scared by so harsh a purity and fled again. The people came and went in fear, and the children did not dare laugh on the street corners. There is no terror greater or colder than the terror of truth.

Justice set up her throne of judgement under a great stone triumphal archway, built to celebrate the conquering of her own distant homeland although she did not know this. She no longer had to go sniffing through the streets, seeking for the smell of exploitation. In their fear the citizens of the Ice City were only too happy to drag out their wrongdoers and submit them to Justice's untender condemnations. Day after day from dawn to dusk she sat there and summarily disposed of all the cases put to her. Her ears received the information and her mouth gave forth their doom. She never hesitated, nor doubted, nor relented. Only at night when she had to sleep alone she was half aware that her skin was dusty and scaled because no one had caressed it. Her dreams were not sweet and it was Neme and the ancestors from far away, not Mercy and Patience, who haunted them. But she would not change her direction because she was without Mercy.

It was a long cold winter.

One day two women came to the seat of judgement under the great archway in the Ice City and asked Justice to judge between them, for their quarrel was between the two of them alone, and it was no one else's concern.

The first woman had a voice as sweet as Mercy's, and Justice could hear her tiredness and sadness, but also her strength and her freedom and her pride. Justice listened to the words of the first woman who said,

'I want to have a abortion and this woman will not let me. It is my body, my right to choose, and I ask for Justice; for life, liberty and the pursuit of happiness.'

Justice grinned. An easy case. But the procedures must be carried through. Although Justice could not see, she must still be seen.

'Well?' she said to the second woman. 'Well, what's your problem?' She paused suddenly, conscious that her ears could not hear the space of the second woman, that her nose could not smell the outline, nor her fingers feel the soft reverberations of presence.

At first there seemed to be no answer. Justice was about to shrug her shoulders, dismiss the case, let the first woman go about her own legitimate business unthreatened by the abstract moralities of another. Then she heard. She had to swivel her great bat-ears, had to lower her head and concentrate to hear the voice of the second woman. The second woman was tiny, maybe ten inches long, and although fur-skinned and fully human she inhabited her world as fish, active, dancing, submerged. Her eyes, like Justice's own, were fused shut, unseeing, and she weighed about ten ounces. It was hard to hear her voice because she spoke from inside the womb of the first woman.

Her voice, as distant as a dream, used a language that ears less attuned than Justice's could not comprehend and she said:

'She does not want to kill me for herself, but for her man. To keep her man's love. She has three daughters already and while she hoped that I would be the son he wants, she was delighted, she fluttered with joy, and I fluttered inside her. Only now she has had the results of the gender test she wants me dead. It is not for life, liberty and the pursuit of happiness; it is for the unjust low esteem that women are held in in the world. It is for servility to her man. I demand Justice, and life, liberty and the pursuit of happiness.'

The first woman said, 'That is all totally irrelevant. It is necessary to my freedom that these arguments be not even heard. I have a right to choose and I wish to exercise it. If it is my right, she cannot be allowed her exceptions.'

The second woman said, 'But it is a right earned only by the real needs of a women. It cannot justly be used against women. How can it be just to destroy a woman-child under circumstances where a man-child would be welcomed? It is the primary, the great discrimination, the heart of injustice.'

And both of them cried out together, 'Justice, Justice, Justice.'

There was a pause. The crowd waited eagerly. The pause

lengthened into a break, a dissonance, a silence. The silence grew longer and longer. The afternoon stopped turning towards evening, held itself ready and waiting. The silence went on and on. And then, nervous, unexpected, tinkling, a child laughed, a laugh as sweet as Mercy's had once been in the long warm evenings on the veranda of the Mission House of Our Lady of the Seven Sorrows. Justice heard the sound, it distracted her. It melted something in her. She knew that she had no right to judge because she had never been where Neme had been; had never held in her hand the tiny foot, paler in the soft unformed arch, redder at the severed ankle, that Neme had found in her hand after the assault on the Village of Lamentation.

She raised her head. The laughing child was hushed and everyone waited on Justice's words.

Justice said,

'I don't know.'

And at once the warm wind kept tightly locked in the deep cupboard was loosed. It came, tickling, tugging, teasing down the streets of the Ice City; it swept away the icicles and they crashed, smashed, dashed, into the streets below. The ice melted like butter on a hob, flowing, glowing, pouring. And all to whom that water came, they cried Alleluia. And were swept up in the great flood of water and wind.

Drenched, dazzled, warm, wet, the first and second woman were whirled away singing to each other.

The first woman sang, 'Of course you can live, delight of my heart.'

The second woman sang, 'Of course you must be free to be joyful, to delight in my sisters who are already born. Of course I am willing to die for so good a cause.'

Suddenly there were buckets and spades in the hands of the children of the Ice City. Suddenly there were piles of coats and gloves and scarves and boots, cast aside and carried off by the flood, the wind, the joy of the new city. Suddenly half the citizens discovered to their surprise that they were wearing bermuda shorts in outrageous acid prints. Suddenly plump pale knees that had not been seen for centuries were being flaunted under the towering glass walls. Sixteen white fluffy clouds performed a delicate minuet in the bright blue sky. The sun roared with laughter and called the moon and the stars to come out and play, and blushed red and gold at their enthusiastic acceptance.

And at last the great warm wind, the great flow of the melting waters, reach high up to Justice's seat of judgement and catch her in their arms. She is tumbled, tossed, by the wind, into the water, and the water bathes her, bathes her eyes until she can see. The warm water flows in at her mouth and out of her ears. The flood laves her, her skin is softened, the scales cream away, she is tender as she has never been. The water plays with her, lifting her high onto frothy waves, and from the topmost curl of one of them the wind snatches her back, swings her high up into the bright sky and she can see all the beauty and the colour of the metamorphozing city. The high buildings of glass and steel melt and tumble into their own crevasses. The ancient buildings of creamy stone resurface, glowing not gleaming. All the old images of power and cruelty are broken, thrown down from their pedestals, cracked and split and destroyed. The blue light of the frost fades, shifts, softens, changes.

Still the wind plays with her, tosses her over and over, till giddy, tumbled, exhausted, she floats, gliding through the air and hears Mercy's voice blending with the singing of the Sisters of the Rose of Sharon, with the drumming of the warm veldt to her own mother's footfalls, and with the perfect music of the nine spheres.

Still the wind takes her. Is she dancing, flying, floating? Is she busy in her balancing? Or is she rather rocked like a baby in the arms of the wind? Justice stretches her eyes until they are as huge and powerful as her ears. She watches from a thousand crazy angles the setting of the sun and the coming of the night. Still through the darkness she is steered by a strength greater than her own, until, just before dawn she feels beneath her a firm footing and stands there erect.

When morning comes the citizens of the new City come out and hurry about their business. It is a gentle day, sunny and springlike. After all the time they have wasted battling the cold they are anxious to get back to their work. Across Holborn Viaduct go the bicyclists, looking down with pleasure on Farringdon Road. Along Fleet Street trot the cleaners, enjoying their new summer clothes, smart and anxious to be back home before their children leave for school. Up Ludgate Hill trundle the big red buses carrying their precious loads. Taxi drivers pour in from Chingford and Leyton, proud of their shiny cabs. It is morning in London, just as always.

Very few people look up and notice that the cross on the very top of what had yesterday been St. Paul's Cathedral has vanished. Now the proud curve of the dome follows perfectly the contours of a woman's breast, offering nourishment, love and security to anyone who wants them.

Very few people look up and notice that just across the street from that loving curve the cold white statue of blind justice, erect, militant, and holding her logical scales, has disappeared. In its place is a small black woman with huge ears, who is holding a balloon. She laughs all the time and never takes her great shining eyes off Mercy's lovely breast.

GENEROSITY

LESLIE DICK

GENEROSITY

Every Indian or other person who engages in or assists in celebrating or encourages either directly or indirectly another to celebrate any Indian festival, dance or other ceremony of which the giving away or paying or giving back of money, goods or articles of any sort forms a part or is a feature, whether such gift of money, goods or articles takes place before, at or after the celebration of the same, or who encourages or assists in any celebration or dance of which the wounding or mutilation of the dead or living body of any human being or animal forms a part or is a feature, is guilty of an offense and is liable on summary conviction for a term not exceeding six months and not less than two months.

Revised Statutes of Canada, 1927, Vol.II, Ch.98, no.140, p.2218

GENEROSITY

Potlatch was first banned by Canadian law in 1884, but this was rarely enforced, partly because the wording of the statute was too vague, and partly because the local magistrates and officials had a relatively tolerant attitude. It stopped completely only during World War I, when the Kwakiutl were instructed by the government agent, 'not to enjoy ourselves while the war was on. We all agree to do as he told us. And had no Potlatch as long as the war was on. And when the war was through we started again.'

Prosecutions followed. Charlie Nowell was sentenced to three months in gaol for giving money to people who came to his brother's funeral. An Indian delegation to Ottawa made no impact. In 1919, in a dramatic courtroom scene, the four accused, as well as seventy-five other men present, agreed to give up the potlatch. In return, the four were given suspended sentences by the government agent, in his role as magistrate and judge. He was aware that sending heads of households to gaol would only produce more families dependent on Indian Agency hand-outs, and no doubt this influenced his decision.

By 1921, the agent was confident that things were once again under control. However, late in the year several more potlatches took place, and then at Christmas he heard about what was rumoured to be the biggest potlatch ever held in the agency. This was Dan Cranmer's potlatch, the 'Christmas Tree' potlatch, which took place at Village Island in Alert Bay. Douglas Cole writes: 'It lasted six days, and involved the giving away of thousands of dollars worth of motor boats, pool tables, sewing machines, gramophones, blankets, flour, and cash.' The local Mounties closed the potlatch down. Twenty-nine Indians, shopped by two who had themselves taken part in the Cranmer potlatch, were prosecuted. The Indians pleaded guilty, and counsel asked for suspended sentences on the grounds that the accused would agree to abstain from potlatch forever.

The Royal Canadian Mounted Police constable objected, pointing out that some of the accused were the very people who'd promised to give up the potlatch in 1919. He insisted on tangible evidence of their reformation, and suggested that the only convincing evidence that was in their power to provide was to 'make a voluntary surrender of all 'Potlach' [sic] coppers, masks, head dresses, Potlach blankets and boxes and all other parpfanalia [sic] used solely for Potlach purposes.' Some of the bands agreed to these terms: The Lekwiltok of Cape Mudge, the Mamalillikulla of Village Island, and the Nimkish of Alert Bay. The people of Turnour Island and Fort Rupert resisted, however, with the result that many of them were sent to prison, including several women, among them a grandmother.

The surrendered potlatch paraphernalia was collected in a woodshed, and then moved to the parish hall in Alert Bay, where it was put on display. It amounted to more than 450 items, including 'twenty coppers, scores of Hamatsa whistles, and dozens of masks'. The government agent wrote: 'It should command good prices for museum purposes.' He was supposed to send it straight to the National Museum in Ottawa, but there was a delay of several months in packing the various things into crates. Meanwhile, in September 1922, GW Heye, one of the most notorious collectors of Indian artefacts, rolled into town, and asked to see the collection. The agent sold Heye thirty-five of the best pieces for $291.

The Department of Indian Affairs and the National Museum were furious when they heard about the sale, especially since the pieces were to be exported to the United States and placed in the Museum of the American Indian, which Heye had founded in 1916. Since the articles were now 'beyond recall', however, they decided to let the matter rest. The remaining material was shipped in seventeen cases to Ottawa, where the appraisal, made by the anthropologist, Edward Sapir, excluding the coppers, came to $1,456. The Indians considered the compensation 'entirely inadequate'. Masks were valued at two to ten dollars (Heye had paid twenty-five for his), and Hamatsa whistles were deemed worth one dollar only. The ceremonial shields, or coppers, were more problematic. Made simply from sheets of copper, each was endowed with its own heraldic pedigree and ritual power, its own soul, so to speak. The value of the coppers was symbolic, or artificial, purely a result of ritual exchange within the social and ceremonial system of Kwakiutl culture. It was impossible, therefore, to estimate an objective monetary value for them. As a result, no compensation was ever paid.

It seems likely that those Indians who cooperated with the police and surrendered various ceremonial items did not hand over everything they owned. The Mounties tactfully refrained from searching people's houses. George Hunt, who worked for many years with the anthropologist Franz Boas, often played the part of middle man between the two communities. (His father was English and had been the Hudson's Bay Company factor at Fort Rupert, and although his mother was a Tlingit, Hunt was raised as a Kwakiutl.) Hunt was employed by Sapir to investigate the genealogy of the surrendered coppers, and he uncovered evidence of a simple sleight-of-hand. While at Kingcombe, he heard that Bob Robertson, owner of the great Loch copper, was telling people that he'd given a facsimile of the Loch to the police, and kept the real thing for himself.

After many years, the coppers came back. In 1979 and 1980, as the outcome of prolonged negotiations, the National Museum in Ottawa, where the collection had remained relatively intact, agreed to return the material to suitable museums established by the Indian communities of Alert Bay and Cape Mudge. It was the first such transfer of this kind.

The thirty-five objects GW Heye purchased for the Museum of the American Indian had a curious history. During the 1940s, many pieces from his vast collection of Northwest Coast artefacts were sold by Heye to the Surrealists, then refugees in New York. Max Ernst, André Breton, Matta, Tanguy, and others, including their friend Lévi-Strauss, became enthusiastic collectors of this work, and Heye, in his position as both founder and director of the Museum, had no qualms about disposing of the very pieces he had so fervently pursued on numerous personal expeditions to the Northwest.

The Surrealists were allowed to browse at their leisure through the vast warehouses of the Museum, located in the Bronx, where the endless shelves and crates loaded with masks and carvings and button blankets called to mind the great potlatches of former times. Heye himself, the bargain hunter *par excellence*, let them have the pieces they selected at cut-rate, not to say giveaway, prices. Thus we see how Kwakiutl masks, confiscated by the Canadian courts, may end up on the living-room walls of Paris intellectuals.

A long time after the diaries incident, maybe two years, Carrie ran into Howard in the street. He was thin and tall, not angular but bowed rather, bending over her slightly as he spoke. Howard showed Carrie his wrist, bony and pale, circled by a bracelet of bright red cotton, knotted simply. He said, 'It's protection: someone's been trying to steal my soul.' Carrie replied, 'It was me. Aeons ago.' He was shocked.

It was when they first met, when she cast that spell, when she was sixteen, and still living with her mother. They'd met before, in London, with the 'gang', when she was fourteeen or so; he'd been fat then, a pale and moon-like face, and he carried with him a small pink toy mouse called Sleep. Everyone had toys or gimmicks, conversation pieces, in those days. She used to carry a metal lunchbox, full of tricks. But this was later, in Ireland, at Sally's house, they met again, and she fell in love.

Carrie'd wanted to fall in love, she was on the lookout for a suitable object. She'd even written in the diary the week before, 'I wonder if I'll fall in love with Howard when he comes' — inky evidence of the inauthenticity of her fall. It was complete. Time passed, and Carrie was in love; she and Howard would stay up all night together, and go out to watch the sun come up over Hampstead Heath, and spend endless afternoons listening to music, smoking dope, hanging out. Clambering over the park railings at 4 a.m., to wake up the ducks at dawn in St James Park, she felt invincible. Paralysed with love, Carrie passed days, and nights, silent, by his side, hoping for a little more. But nothing ever happened.

Meanwhile Carrie was going to school every day, hating her teachers, getting into trouble, bunking off, and compulsively talking to her friends. Schoolgirls still, the elaborate vocabulary of adolescent romance was called upon to make sense of their all too serious love affairs. It was around this time that she made friends with Jo. Compulsive, she spoke of him, an incessant interpretation of incidents, hearsay, phone calls, constantly going over the evidence to produce an answer to one question: does he love me? Jo listened, taking it all in. Carrie told stories, as if a line, a rope, a sequence could hold it all, could account for this emotional turmoil. Jo, self-contained, kept her thoughts and feelings close, planted like seeds. Carrie was scattered and desperate, and then suddenly quiet when she was with him.

Carrie was reading Frazer's *Golden Bough*, more or less because she wanted to understand Eliot, and Modernism, and late one night she found a spell. It was a spell to be performed under a red moon, in Malaya, by those who want their love returned. Carrie was sitting crouched on her narrow bed, in the little attic room she lived in at the top of her mother's house. There was a very large Beardsley poster on the wall beside the bed, and over her head, as a wry comment on her virginity, she'd stuck a *News of the World* placard, a crude banner headline that read: MY WILD NIGHTS WITH THE MAD AXEMAN.

Next door to her white room was a narrow bathroom, with a small casement window that opened onto a parapet. If you were willing to risk death, a drop of five storeys, it was possible to clamber out of the bathroom window, and step from the parapet diagonally across onto the small flat roof of the back extension. The July night that Carrie was reading *The Golden Bough*, as she got to the bit about soul-catching, and the red moon low over the eastern horizon, she looked out of the window and saw, for the first time in this city, a huge fat red moon, lying low in the dark sky. Without hesitation, she carefully re-read the spell, and got up off the bed to climb out of the bathroom window onto the roof. She had never before carried out this delicate operation at night. The red full moon was uncanny, an unexpected gift.

Holding the thick paperback in her hands, her long hair falling down her back, face turned up towards the moon, Carrie repeated the words, following the directions 'for securing the soul of one whom you wish to render distraught'.

I loose my shaft, I loose it and the moon clouds over,
I loose it, and the sun is extinguished.
I loose it, and the stars burn dim.
But it is not the sun, moon, and stars that I shoot at,
It is the stalk of the heart of that child, So-and-so.

Cluck! cluck! soul of So-and-so, come and walk with me.
Come and sit with me,
Come and sleep and share my pillow.
Cluck! cluck! soul.

Somebody at sunrise be distraught for love of me,
Somebody at sunset be distraught for love of me,
As you remember your parents, remember me;
As you remember your house and house-ladder,
    remember me;
When thunder rumbles, remember me;
When wind whistles, remember me;
When the heavens rain, remember me;
When the cocks crow, remember me;

When you look up at the sun, remember me;
When you look up at the moon, remember me;
For in that self-same moon I am there.
Cluck! cluck! soul of Somebody come hither to me.
I do not mean to let you have my soul,
Let your soul come hither to mine.

The spell worked. Only a few weeks later, he took her hand and kissed it, sitting on the floor at her feet very late at night, and she leaned forward, bending down over his upturned face, to kiss his lips. Months passed; in his bookshelf, Carrie found the very same edition of *The Golden Bough*, a fat paperback with its spine uncreased, and she wrote his initials HWS in fine pencil in the margin beside the spell. She wanted to be found out, some day; it was a dead giveaway.

In the street, all these years later, Howard looked at her with mild horror. Carrie thought, he's been to India now, he's finally getting around to reading Frazer. Howard explained how he'd found the counter-spell, the red thread tied around the wrist, in the same chapter. 'Jo said she thought it was you,' he muttered. Carrie laughed, defiant, at last: 'She was right!'

Carrie remembered Jo on the beach, in Dorset, taking off her clothes to go swimming and expressing with annoyance how clumsy she felt, how uncomfortable she was, undressed. She was seventeen, then. Jo was beautiful, she had a kind of pent-up fierceness inside her, that emerged in gestures of irritation or dismissal. Her face was like a Spanish saint. Her hand, moving, would convey the aggression her body contained; she stood firm on the ground, immovable, like a heifer, or a young bull.

Carrie remembered another time, a couple of years later, Jo asking her, suddenly, 'Do you have orgasms?' She'd been a little shaken, and answered yes, automatically. It turned out Jo didn't, with Howard, and wondered if Carrie did, or had. 'No, not with

Howard.' 'When, then?' 'Well, masturbating . . .' 'Oh,' Jo said, her hands making a gesture of dismissal, 'masturbation's not a problem.' She produced a leaflet called *The Myth of the Vaginal Orgasm*, and Carrie read it, amazed. She'd never talked about this stuff before.

Later Howard worked it into his stand-up comedy routine; he'd sing a song, in the persona of a rather lame new man type, about a meaningful relationship where he went out with a woman for four years and she never had an orgasm. The audience roared. Howard became a famous comedian, eventually; she'd see him on TV occasionally, by chance.

Much later, in New York, Carrie found herself in a half-empty movie theatre one afternoon, watching *Brazil*, with her friend Louise. Without warning, Howard appeared on the screen, momentarily, for one short gag, just time for Carrie to point and cry out, '*That's* the first man I ever slept with!' 'Which one?' 'Him! Him! There!' she shrieked, whispering, while the rest of the scattered audience started to rustle and snicker.

Finally, something like twelve or fifteen years later, she saw Jo across a crowded room at an opening at the Hayward, and at first she thought Jo was cutting her. This was intolerable, so Carrie went up to say hello. Bill was standing next to her. Carrie said, warmly, 'I hear you've had a baby, congratulations!' And Jo pointed to her stomach and said, 'Another one on the way.' Laughing, Carrie said, 'Oh I'm envious, I want one of them.' Whereupon Jo looked hard at her and said, dubiously, 'Why would *you* want to have a baby?' That did it, finally. Looking at Jo, her attachment unfolded, turning inside out. Carrie had nothing to say.

The night he told her, the night he illuminated her darkness, untied the knots of confusion, exposing a landscape of utter devastation, that night was seared into Carrie's mind, burned into her like blinding flares slow falling in a black sky.

In the morning Howard called her up, asked her over, to spend the day. This hadn't happened in a very long time. (Later, she would realise that Jo must have put him up to it, she must have said, 'You have to tell her. She doesn't know, she hasn't guessed. You have to tell her this weekend.') Carrie was terribly pleased that he'd called, that he'd pursued her, for once. He was living in Oxford, going to college, and she was still at school in London, that was one reason they didn't see each other much. Lately, however, when they spent time together, Jo was there, or other people, his younger brother's friends, and things were strained and difficult. Typically Carrie didn't question this; she imagined the strain must somehow be her fault, that she wasn't pleasing him in some way. She hoped it would go away, hoping like holding your breath and closing your eyes and wishing this unpleasure would somehow fade. The ostrich position? Meanwhile, she stayed quiet, keeping her head down, so she wouldn't have to see, she wouldn't have to feel the slap in the face.

She never questioned this, accepting it all as part of being in love, the price of being allowed to spend time with him. It was as if she had no rights, no claim on anyone, no expectations. She couldn't say, 'Don't treat me this way.' One time she worked up her courage to telephone and she dialled his number and laughing he told her that Jo was there and they were pretending it was a power cut (it was a winter of power cuts, the miners were bringing the Tory government down, people took baths by candlelight and talked about how it was like Dickens), that evening Jo and Howard were pretending, they were lighting candles together, playing at power cuts. Carrie winced inside, unable even to acknowledge it to herself. She was scared to death, and didn't know it.

That day, the day Howard called, Saturday, Carrie put on a red dress, and she washed her hair, and then she got on the bus for the long ride to his house, his parents' house. It was sunny, mid-February, a clear cold day with the pale sunlight of English winters. She was friendly with his mother, who was also called Carrie. That day, his mother was particularly sweet to her, and

Howard became impatient. They went out, Hampstead Heath was nearby, and they went there, as they always did. He was so nice to her, talking and paying attention to her only. Carrie was quietly ecstatic. She was used to doing whatever he wanted her to to do, appearing when he asked her to, going home when he wanted her to leave, fucking him, or not, as he chose. She accepted this lavish attention now with silent amazement, it seemed an unlooked-for gift from the gods.

They sat on the low bough of an ancient tree, and he told her how he had a weapon against her, there was something he had to tell her, he had this weapon against her and he had to give it up. Carrie insisted on remaining completely oblivious to this threat. She wasn't curious, she affected a profound detachment from such unpleasantness. Idealistic, she didn't want to know. She kept saying, 'Forget it, don't worry about it. It's such a lovely day, don't ruin it.' And he went on clutching his head and saying, 'There's something I have to tell you.' And she kept smiling gently and floating airily through the park, saying, 'Stop worrying, forget it.'

In this way the whole day passed, until finally, late at night, they went back to her place, to climb into her narrow bed with the bright yellow sheets and make love once more. It was two in the morning when he finally said it, when he finally managed to say the fatal words: 'There's someone else.' Later Carrie figured he must have promised himself, or Jo, that he'd tell her before the day was out; cowardly, he'd left it to the last possible minute, so late at night, and really a lousy moment, post-coital, but at least he managed to get the words out of his mouth.

Her first response was to sustain her pose of total disinterest, airy detachment. She immediately envisaged the Other Woman, a blonde girl called something like Diane, or Suzette, even, a blonde with painted fingernails and eye makeup. It was a vision of everything she wasn't, a cliché of sexiness against which she, Carrie, could play soulmate. Carrie's implicit, unspoken line on this was: 'I can take anything you've got to give, nothing you can do or say can change my love for you, and while you're at it, please don't drag me into the ghastly details of your little peccadilloes, please, my love for you is far far above all this.'

So at first she said nothing, lying flat on her back naked in the narrow bed, so close to his long body. Her eyes were focused on nothing, some point in the middle distance above her head. He said, 'There's someone else.' She said nothing. She absented herself from this conversation. It was a pretty effective tactic, she could see that it upset him. He pressed her, he said, 'You have to help me, please, help me to tell you. I've got to tell you. Please, ask me questions.' Submissive in all things, Carrie did not speak her mind (she really didn't want to know), instead she lay there and tried to think of a question to ask. There was nothing she wanted to know. She thought of the most innocuous, least informative question she could ask, a question that took it for granted that she'd never met this other woman. She said, 'OK. What's her name?' Howard hesitated, then he said, 'You know.'

Shock flooded her body, like a bright light suddenly switched on. It was Jo, of course, and suddenly everything made sense. Carrie was shocked to the bone. She wanted to talk to her right away. It was too late at night to phone. Somewhere she had always known, yet she'd never suspected, even remotely. Carrie had nothing whatsoever to say to Howard. She felt this was between her and Jo, Howard was irrelevant, almost, or unimportant. She didn't want to talk about it with him, she didn't really want to have anything to do with him. She'd never told him how much she loved him, she'd hidden all that, absolutely certain the ludicrous extent of her adoration would be totally unacceptable. He didn't know what he'd done. But Jo knew. Carrie had told Jo everything.

As the night passed it became clear that Howard seemed to think they could go on as before, that the problem had been Carrie's innocence, or ignorance, her terrible vulnerability. He didn't want to have to choose between them. That was intolerable to him. He refused this position of power. He didn't want to hurt her, or Jo, he didn't want to stop seeing either of them. They were free. Eyes open wide, Carrie still had nothing to say. The one she wanted to talk to was Jo. She was reeling from the double shock: the sexual betrayal, the humiliating realization of her own blindness. There was nothing left. She didn't sleep very well.

In the morning she rang Jo as early as possible. She said 'Please come round. I want to talk to you.' Jo gave out a sort of shrieking giggle, most uncharacteristic, and Carrie realised with surprise that Jo must be nervous, even scared of her. Carrie was playing to an internal audience, it was epic operatic tragic drama she was enacting, and they were nervous? This was annoying. Carrie felt that she was rising to the occasion, so to speak, or maybe dragging the somewhat paltry and banal occasion up closer to her high ideals. She hoped Jo and Howard wouldn't let her down.

What happened then was Howard wouldn't leave. He understood that Jo was coming round, to talk to Carrie, and he wouldn't leave. He hung around, playing the guitar. Carrie was distraught, silent, even beginning to feel glimmers of anger. Finally she asked him to go. He stayed. Later she guessed or recognized that he was madly in love with Jo, and thus compelled perhaps to take every chance of a few moments with her. She was perplexed. Then there was the horrible possibility that Jo had arranged this with him, fixed it so that she, Jo, wouldn't be left alone with Carrie's possible wrath. Carrie felt nauseous.

Eventually, Jo appeared, nervous, and like lovers do, their eyes locked, Jo and Howard sat down close together, they couldn't resist touching each other, and they ignored Carrie. Maybe they really were scared of her, of what she'd say. Or maybe this was the moment of truth, representing some kind of commitment to this until now more or less illicit or undercover romance. Calculating back to the evening in Richmond when Jo told Carrie she was thinking of going on the pill, and wouldn't say why, Carrie guessed they'd been sleeping together for about two and a half months. Carrie sensed they were protecting themselves against her, and she felt upset that she should seem so threatening, when she was the one who'd been wronged. They even looked alike, Howard and Jo: pale skin, dark hair, long narrow eyes.

Again, Carrie asked Howard to go. He left, reluctantly. Possibly he was squeamish about what these two would say about him now that they both knew what he'd been doing, what they'd say behind his back. Carrie didn't care, that wasn't the issue. The issue for Carrie was straightforward: how could Jo keep her in the dark for so long?

Years later, it was the fried eggs she remembered, the eggs she fried to give to Jo and Howard the morning Jo got back from the States. Carrie had been lying in bed with Howard that morning, his long, pale body, warm skin so close in the big bed. She'd been lying in his arms, her ex-boyfriend's arms, where she wanted to be, when the doorbell rang, too early in the morning. (She'd moved out of her mother's house, by then, she was living with her sister, Tina.) Carrie had no recollection of throwing a dressing-gown on, walking barefoot down the icy hall to the front door, only the unspeakable shock when the door opened to reveal Jo — Jo back, unannounced, unexpected — Jo, straight from the airport, with some guy in tow, a bearded hippy she'd met on the plane.

They'd come straight from the airport; the hippy was coming down off acid; but none of this registered, what registered was the (mistaken) idea that Jo had come to Carrie's house because she (inexplicably) knew Howard was there. Carrie didn't question this idea (it made no sense), later she realised it was because she felt bad about sleeping with Howard while Jo was away. Despite everything, Carrie insisted on continuing to think of Jo as one of her dearest friends. She'd given them her blessing, she'd given up, and therefore she felt she really shouldn't fall into bed with Howard when Jo wasn't around. Nevertheless, when Howard came after her, when he came knocking on her door late at night, unannounced, unexpected, after Jo left for the States, Carrie would take him gladly into her bed, wrap her smooth body around him, and feel badly, a horrible little black scrap of bad feeling, about Jo.

So it was frighteningly appropriate, that on one of these mornings (he only slept with her three or maybe four times in the three weeks Jo was away, although once he showed up when she was in bed with Jo's brother, Philip, and maybe he would have stayed the night if she hadn't been), on one of these blissful mornings of re-possession, with Howard still asleep in the big bed, it seemed almost appropriate that Carrie should open the door and find Jo. And believe, unquestioning, that Jo knew Howard was there.

There was a moment of pure confusion, when it became clear that Jo didn't know. Carrie remembered the tiny contortions of her face, as Jo took in the fact that he was here, that Carrie thought she knew he was here, and implicitly, that Carrie had probably been lying in bed with him only moments before. All this took place on the doorstep, and then Jo, decisive, moved directly down the corridor to the bedroom, while Carrie showed the tripping hippy to the floor cushions in the front room, and asked him if he wanted anything, some orange juice, or what. He wanted to crash out.

She went back down the hall, and saw Jo, radiantly happy, clambering into the bed, with her clothes on, and Howard, also looking completely blissed out, kissing her shoulder, gently, looking like he always did when he woke up, bemused and wondering.

Carrie's automatic response to this unspeakably painful scene was to worry that Jo might be hurt or upset, might think she'd been sleeping with Howard. It was her sister's bed, the big bed (Tina was away) that Howard was lying naked in, and just conceivably Carrie might have slept in her own bed, the bed in the front room, and put Howard in the big bed, if he'd come round then stayed too late to drive home. Anxious, Carrie wanted to protect Jo from realizing what had happened; she hoped she wouldn't notice the two pillows, side by side, the dent she'd left in her sleep. Carrie almost succeeded in thinking she was pleased to see Jo, pleased to see the two of them so happy. The only thing she wasn't quite up for was the hippy stranger, sprawled across the floor cushions, sound asleep.

So she had no place to be; there were only two rooms in this flat, the bedroom at the back, and the front room, her room, where she usually slept; Carrie had no place to be, so she decided to make breakfast. She vanished into the very small kitchen. She fried two eggs, in butter. They were pale and smooth, without colour, and she put them on a large white plate, alone. She didn't make toast; they were out of bread.

She took this flat white plate with its shiny flat white eggs into the bedroom, the fried eggs sliding slightly on the surface of the plate, she took them in to give to Howard and Jo. They looked up at her from their absorbed embrace, eyes locked in passionate rediscovery, they looked up at her, distractedly, as if surprised that anyone else existed in the world. She gave them the plate with the two eggs on it, and two forks, recognizing for the first time that this breakfast really wasn't very appetizing. It was more like a gesture, this gift, a representation of a good breakfast: eggs. Really it wasn't very nice. Carrie retreated once more, leaving them to it.

She opened the french windows that led from the front room down the side of the house to the garden at the back, and sat down on the step, her elbows propped on her knees, holding her head. It was wearing, this; she felt worn out. A while later the hippy surfaced and volunteered the information that tripping out on long flights was really the best place to do acid because he'd realized the only real problem, on acid, was having to make decisions. And on a plane, there are no decisions to make. You just sit in your seat for eight hours. Eliminate alternatives to avoid a bad trip.

Carrie had so far successfully managed to avoid all hallucinogenic drugs, despite the fact that almost everyone she knew dropped acid regularly. Nevertheless, she harboured a soft spot for the fantasy of tripping out on pure organic mescalin, some day, in nature, in a lovely park on a sunny day, some time. The idea of doing acid inside the plastic environment of a transatlantic jet was completely uncongenial to her. She hated flying anyway. What if you did have a bad trip? There would be nowhere to go. Hell. Stuck in a nightmare. Not so very dissimilar to the predicament she found herself in now.

I think I've forgotten everything I knew about potlatch. I always forget. I can't even remember the plot of a novel unless I've read it nineteen times. I read all those potlatch books last year and they all started to merge into each other.

The one I liked best wasn't really about potlatch at all. It was about this man called William Duncan of Metlakatla, Metlakatla was the utopian community he founded. He was a missionary, from England, Lincolnshire, I think, working-class background, mid-nineteenth century, he was an apprentice, and he read all these improve yourself books, anyway, eventually he became a missionary and was sent out to British Columbia to save the Indians, the Tsimshian. And what was so annoying and perplexing to all the British missionaries and the upright proper merchants and all the colonialists, was what a fine old time the Indians in BC were having without having to do any of what they would call real work. The whole ethic of work and save and suffer and pray and die and go to heaven, the whole thing was completely irrelevant to these people. They were rich, they lived well, they always had plenty to eat, endless salmon and oolachan, and lots of leisure time, so an enormous part of their culture was about games and rituals, literally thinking up things to do in the winter months when the snows came. Even war for them was a kind of huge game, all revolving around the question of status. It was all about showing off.

So the big problem the missionaries faced was how to persuade these people to give up this rather pleasant life, to abandon their extremely elaborate mythology and religion and structures of ritual and family and everything, to make them so to speak buckle under and face the fact that we're put here on earth to suffer, and Jesus died for our sins, and the wages of sin is death, and we're all going to die. All that. And work, they had to make them work. And live in separate houses — the Kwakiutl and the Tsimshian and the Haida all lived in big wooden houses, beautifully painted, thirty or forty people in each, and these buildings were really ideal for the constant parties and elaborate plays and performances and all the socializing they went in for. And the potlatch. Most of all, they had to stop the potlatch. It was the key issue really, to get them to accept a (literally) capitalist economy, an economy of saving and investment and labour and just rewards in heaven, to get them to stop giving everything away! Anyway, William Duncan tried and tried, and also of course there was the struggle against liquor and prostitution and all the sinful activity that contact with the Europeans introduced. Particularly alcohol.

Eventually Duncan realized that the only way to get them to forsake their culture, and to protect them from the temptations of the local fort, was to remove them from it entirely, i.e. to build a new village, where everything would be organized along Christian principles. Where he would be the sole arbiter of Christian economics and moral behaviour. He was greatly helped in this project by a massive smallpox epidemic that swept through the Indian communities, moving north up the coast from Victoria, wiping out thousands — many of them, it goes without saying, already considerably weakened by venereal disease which they'd acquired through prostituting the women in Victoria and Prince Rupert and Fort Simpson. Needless to say, Duncan had no hesitation in depicting this epidemic as a scourge from heaven, and lots of lost people were recruited to the new village out of sheer desperation and grief. Maybe a few hundred, to begin with; there were almost a thousand at its height.

And they set off and built Metlakatla, the city on the hill, and William Duncan ruled it like an absolute monarch, making up rules and regulations and punishments, the carrot and the stick, to cajole and enforce his ideas of propriety. After a few years there was gossip in Victoria that he was fucking the young women, and certainly it was true that he beat them severely for relatively minor misdemeanours. He used to lock them up in the cupboard under the stairs.

By this time he wasn't on good terms with the Anglican church establishment in Canada or England, nor with the Missionary Society. And there was some fracas, another churchman appeared, he sneaked in while William Duncan was away, and he gave a rousing sermon on the mystic powers of the Holy Ghost, whereupon the Metlakatla people started having visions and seeing signs, and crying out in frenzy, and a bunch of them stayed up all night praying and heard the voice of the Holy Spirit itself. And Duncan heard about this down in Victoria, and he hightailed it back up to Metlakatla, which was pretty remote, and then basically he punished these people for days until they finally admitted that their visions and aural hallucinations (which of course were particularly dangerous because they weren't so very different from the kind of ecstatic states Duncan associated with their own religion), these visions were a snare and a delusion, and the work of the devil, and it was back to the Duncan line on all of this, which was pretty fucking minimal. Like for example, Duncan never let them celebrate communion, he never told them about it, transubstantiation, because it was too close to their religion. It was as if he wanted to abolish all traces of metaphor, and any kind of extreme spiritual state, and all rituals of performance, to distance the Anglican church as much as possible from the Winter Dances and the great potlatches of former times. On the other hand, he let them put up carved totem poles on either side of the altar in one of the chapels. So it wasn't simple.

What was interesting about Metlakatla was this kind of compromise, in all the practical stuff, like what to wear. It's always the same problem for these missionaries: how to get people to give up their comfortable and efficient clothes, for uncomfortable and inefficient and expensive European dress. And the problem of architecture, to get them to give up their communal houses. They came to a compromise on the houses by sort of shoving the two styles together. They'd build two conventional anglo-style houses, with two storeys, and separate rooms, etc., and then on the ground floor a great room to connect the two houses, with a fire burning in it, so you could still hang out together, in one great long smoky room. But you slept in a proper, private space.

Also Duncan was very business-minded, and into manufacturing whatever there was a market for, including tourist artefacts. They all did it, all the different bands made stuff to sell to the foreigners, from really early on, but it was particularly striking at Metlakatla because they'd made such an effort to impose European standards of dress and cleanliness and punctuality and privacy. And then years pass and Duncan is getting the old women to teach the young women how to make the traditional head-dresses out of bark, so that he can sell them down at Fort Simpson. Getting them to remember the things he'd tried so hard to make them forget.

I don't remember it very clearly. I know it was dark, when they came, it was late, and I think they telephoned first, I think it was Jo on the phone, saying, 'We want to come round, is that all right?' And of course I said yes, because I said yes to everything, it was the easiest thing to do. Or maybe I said yes because I wanted to see them, to see him, to see her. I don't know. I was going to school every day, they weren't. By that time Howard was dropping out of college, and Jo hadn't started yet, she was doing her ritual year off before university, the year in which you were meant to travel, to hitch around the US, or take the overland route to India.

In any case I remember it was dark when they came, and I guess I was alone, I don't know where Tina was, maybe she was out, I don't know. It wasn't very long after the whole debacle, the extraordinary renunciation I'd made, this moment when I'd broken the triangle, I'd said, 'Oh OK, go.' I'd said, 'I don't want to play any more.' I'd said, 'He's all yours.' Somehow during this time I'd salvaged something from the wreckage, an image of myself, some kind of narrative in which I starred, pale and wan, the classic victim of a broken heart, magnanimously giving up the man she loves to the woman who's betrayed her. See, I could have fought for him; I could at least have made their lives a misery. I could have made bitter accusations. But I didn't. I was proud, I was generous, and I behaved impeccably.

Anyway it wasn't very long after all this drama, and we were all three of us busy fervently pretending that there wasn't a problem, that we could still continue to be friends. At least that's what I was doing. So I was slightly surprised to find how much tension there was when they walked in, when they entered this little front room where we'd all spent so much time separately and together, where the love affair had taken place and where my heart had been broken. They came in, and I do remember that they didn't seem to find it easy to be together in front of me, which I guess isn't that surprising, but still I think that was more Howard than Jo, Jo wanted things to be clear, I think, whereas Howard felt guilty and also perhaps he wanted me still. I don't know. I mean, when she went to the States he used to come and sleep with me, I didn't know what that was about. I liked it though, sleeping with him, I mean fucking him, and sleeping with him. I was in love with him still, I guess.

So anyway that night they weren't really very much at ease, you know, and neither was I, but I was always taking up this position of fearlessness, I think it was my mother's training, I could always pull it out of the hat, this sort of social ease, this savoir-faire. In any case, I was able to seem more at ease than they were, although I'm sure I was in crisis inside. And so they didn't sit down or anything like that, I remember Howard sort of wandered off to the far side of the room, in the darkness, and I sat at the table by the lamp. The walls of that room were bright yellow, like a Vuillard, and the corners were in dark shadow. There was a very large mirror over the mantlepiece above the square table, it reflected the yellow light. Howard was standing aimlessly in the darkness, and Jo said, 'We've come to read your diaries.'

I wrote diaries then, every day before I went to sleep I wrote down everything that happened. And ever since I'd fallen in love with Howard I had written as the last words of each daily entry, 'I love Howard.' Or: 'I love you.' In retrospect it seems very adolescent, but then I was sixteen, or seventeen by then, which is adolescent, and maybe that's when you define yourself in those kinds of terms: I am the one who loves Howard. Howard is who I love. I love Howard. And of course the diaries contained multitudinous secrets, endless petty gripes and nastinesses, all the detritus of daily life, my ugly feelings, that ended up in this secret waste disposal unit, page after page covered in black scribble. And the notebooks: I kept a daily journal, or diary, a record of events, and in tandem I wrote in big black notebooks, I wrote the excess, what wouldn't fit, great splurges of emotion and analysis — what I would now call analysis. So I was pretty shocked when Jo said, 'We've come to read your diaries.'

To me the diaries, the notebooks were by definition unread able. They were my secret, my most precious object. No one could read them. Yet I don't remember even hesitating. I don't remember taking a minute to consider refusing them this request. Trying to be casual, in a gesture of complete abjection, I said, 'But of course!' I went to the place where I kept the books, and I said, 'Which ones do you want?' Jo said, 'This year, and last year. And the notebooks.' And I handed them over.

The two of them sat down at the table, and it was my turn to stand around the room aimlessly. Sidelong, I watched them turn the pages. I remember sensing a certain embarrassment on Howard's part, as if he didn't really want to be doing this to me. But it was also like a scene in a Resistance movie, this extraordinary moment, when they divided the diaries between them. Jo took this year's, Howard took last year, in order to find out my secrets. I thought, 'I've got nothing left to lose.' I think it must have been a shock to Howard to read those three words, 'I love Howard', ending each scrawled entry, since I'd never said it to him directly. I thought he wouldn't like it. I remember he started to read and then obviously sickened of this task, he resorted to merely leafing through, glancing at things as they struck his eye. Jo was more systematic; I think she was looking for stuff I'd written about her.

I'd been seeing her brother, Philip, we'd been dating, or something like that, in some crazed and complicated scenario of revenge and substitution. As I said at the time to Nina, our mutual friend, I said, 'Well obviously it goes without saying that the nearest I can get to fucking Jo is to fuck Philip.' Nina was a little shocked, I think. Also I have to admit that I'd always suspected that Jo wanted to sleep with her brother, and couldn't, whereas I could, and did. I liked Philip, but the situation was so over-determined it wasn't really possible for us to find or make a relation that was our own, to say the least, so we gave up on it pretty quickly. Also I'd come off the pill, another gesture of abnegation, as if renouncing my claims on Howard meant giving up sex altogether. We tended to be slightly puritanical in those days about the pill; we thought you should start taking it when you entered into a serious relationship, that somehow being on it all the time was a sign of being a bit too loose, or easygoing. And we were terribly *sérieuse*.

In any case I never got any contraceptives together when I was seeing Philip, so we'd have these slightly contorted sexual encounters, and though he was very beautiful and very lovely — he had lovely long eyes and very soft skin, just like Jo's — it really didn't work. Anyway, when Jo was reading my diary she finally found something to point to, she pointed her finger to the words: 'Philip says Jo is a tough cookie.' I remember the other thing Philip said was, 'I don't know how people like Howard can exist.' I think she was a little disappointed.

My suspicion was that she wanted to prove something to

Howard, and that was hard for me to imagine. I mean at the time I didn't picture them spending their time talking about me and what I felt and what I meant to them, but of course that's what they did. I was much more important to them than I ever let myself imagine. And then of course I'd confided in Jo, I'd told her (almost) everything (I didn't talk about sex with her, but then I didn't talk about sex with anyone at all then), most of all I'd told her over and over again how passionate I was about Howard, and how beautiful I found him and on and on and on. The things I felt I was forbidden to say to him. And she must have been trying to get Howard to see this, because he'd refused to — I'd kept this overwhelming passion carefully hidden from him, knowing it would scare him to death. He was skittish enough anyway, and he seemed to want me to be very cool, and I wanted to be what he wanted me to be, so I was very cool, very undemanding, very detached. I never said I love you, I never said, your beautiful eyes, your lovely neck, your pale skin. I never said those things. And he never said them to me.

So I think that the whole project of 'reading the diaries' was to demonstrate to Howard the extreme discrepancies between my silence and my emotion. To make it clear to him that I was madly in love, and thus to shift his perception of me, to make him want to get away from me, even. That's what I suspected, later, anyway. And I colluded with Jo in this, in some way I invited their invasion, and I think it was insane that I let them do it. Because no one had ever read my notebooks and diaries before, and it turned out that I could write them only if I was certain of their inviolability. This act of reading demolished that once and for all. Empty-handed, I stopped writing altogether.

What I do remember is that after Jo left for the States (which wasn't very long afterwards) Howard asked me round to his house, his parents' house, and he took me up to his little room and sat me down at the desk with its white formica top where once I wrote a line in pencil, a backhanded declaration of love, he took me up to this room where we'd spent so much time and taken drugs and where he'd fucked me for the first time, where I'd lost my virginity, that is, and he opened one of the drawers in the desk and brought out a few sheets of paper and he said, 'I wanted to give you these, to make it equal, because I've read your stuff now, so you can read this.' And then he looked at one of them, and said, 'Oh no, not this one!' and laughed, and he put that one back in the drawer, and then he said, 'I'll go out for a while, now,' and he left me with two or three poems he'd written about me when we were going out together. And they were very beautiful, and I wished I'd known about them before.

And then, of course, I opened the drawer and I read the one that I wasn't supposed to read, which was a poem that compared me and Jo, unfavourably. He described my miserable face, puffy with depression and flu, and then the thrill and pleasure of seeing her, surrounded by colours, in the artists' materials shop where she was working. Needless to say this poem managed to undo any pleasure I might have had in the love poems he'd given me to read. I remember it ended with an expression of disgust, 'ugh!' he wrote, and I was devastated. Later I told Nina about it, and she said she thought the 'ugh!' was quite funny, it was so desperate and so extreme. But when your lover writes 'ugh!' about you when you're seventeen it isn't very funny really. Now it's kind of a scream, sort of.

Kwakiutl coppers were useless and very beautiful objects, not unlike a shield, made of rolled and beaten copper. In Kwakiutl culture during the nineteenth and early twentieth centuries, the copper was the most precious thing one could possess.

Coppers are vaguely oblong in shape, usually about eighteen inches long, curving at the apex, with sides narrowing at an angle from the top to the middle part, and then diverging slightly or staying parallel below. The upper portion is often engraved with the image of a face, while the lower rectangle has only two perpendicular ridges, making a T-shape across the lower half. It is a complex shape, which Lévi-Strauss describes as 'enigmatic'.

The copper from which these objects were made may have originally come from Indian bands in Alaska, but by 1800 it was intermittently available through trading with the Europeans, who carried sheets of it to repair leaks in their ships. According to Marcel Mauss, the mythological sequence goes: springtime, arrival of salmon, new sun, red colour, copper.

Each copper had a name, for example: Sea Lion, Killer Whale, Noisy Copper, Quarrel Maker, Moon, All Other Coppers are Ashamed to Look at It. Thus the coppers are 'like' a man (with a face and a name, and a body traced in the T-shape), like a salmon, like the sun after the winter ice, like life. Coppers were useful solely as representations of wealth; they could be bought and sold, cut up into pieces, broken in the fire, or, most dramatically, thrown into the sea.

Coppers were central to the culture of the potlatch. In order to humiliate the other, one is generous to him. To shame him, one showers him with objects, one 'buys' his copper. The copper then represents the excessive liberality of the chief who thus acquired it; a copper's value is measured by rivalry. To reduce the other to a state of abjection, one destroys objects of value, coppers, throwing them away.

Mauss records, quoting Boas, that in 1910, the copper Lesaxalayo was worth 9,000 woollen blankets (each worth about $4), 50 canoes, 6,000 button blankets (red and blue flannel blankets with mass-produced mother-of-pearl buttons sewn all over them in elaborate patterns), 260 silver bracelets, 60 gold bracelets, 70 gold ear-rings, 40 sewing machines, 25 gramophones, and 50 masks.

George Hunt recounts the true story of two Kwakiutl chiefs, who were great friends, called Fastrunner and Throwaway. Throwaway invited the clan of his friend to a feast of salmon berries, but he carelessly served the oil and berries in dishes that weren't perfectly clean. Fastrunner was offended; he refused the food, and lay down with his black bear blanket drawn over his face. All his relatives, seeing these signs of his displeasure, followed his example. Whereupon Throwaway urged them to eat, and the ceremonial speaker replied: 'Our chief will not eat the dirty things you have offered, O dirty man.' Throwaway was offended in his turn, and said: 'You speak as if you were a person of very great wealth.' This was equivalent to throwing down the gauntlet. Fastrunner replied, 'Indeed I am,' and sent his runners to bring his copper, Sea Monster. Fastrunner pushed the copper into the fire, in order 'to put out the fire of his rival'. This gesture of destruction must be matched, and Throwaway sent for his copper, called Looked at Askance, and he too pushed it into the fire, 'to keep it burning'. But Fastrunner had another copper, Crane, and he sent for that and placed it upon the fire, 'to smother it.' Throwaway was thus defeated, having no other copper to destroy.

However the next day, to carry this scene of rivalry and humiliation to its conclusion, Fastrunner returned the feast, and sent his attendants to invite Throwaway and all his relatives. In the night, Throwaway had feverishly pledged enough property to borrow another copper. So when the feast began, he refused to eat (using the same words which Fastrunner had used the day before) and sent his runners to bring the copper Day Face. He laid this on the fire, and extinguished it. Fastrunner rose and spoke: 'Now is my fire extinguished. Wait; sit down and see the deed that I shall do.' He 'put on the excitement' of the Dance of Fools (the secret society of which he was a member) and he sent for four canoes, belonging to his father-in-law. These canoes were heaped on the fire in the feasting-house, to take away the shame of having their fire extinguished. The flames were terrifying, fuelled by lashings of oolachan fish grease, yet Fastrunner's guests had to remain sitting there, or admit defeat. The black bear blanket of Throwaway was scorched, and under the blanket the skin of his legs blistered, but he sat tight. When the blaze diminished, he arose as if nothing had happened, and took some food as if to demonstrate his complete indifference to the extravagance of his rival.

These gestures of waste, sacrifice, and rivalry escalated between the two chiefs, until finally Fastrunner killed a slave. The body of the slave was cut up by the Fool Dancers and the Grizzly Bear Society, and then apparently eaten by the Hamatsa. The scalp he gave to Throwaway, who could not match this mighty deed. Later Throwaway and his warriors set forth on a warlike expedition against another band, and none of them returned. As Ruth Benedict writes: 'The characteristic Kwakiutl response to frustration was sulking and acts of desperation.'

One day Carrie came home from school and found signs that someone, some foreign body, had been in the flat. Tina was in Italy at the time, staying with their mother. They always left the front window unlocked, in case someone was late or forgot their keys; it was very easy to clamber over the sill. First she found a teapot, cold tea, and a dirty cup in the sink. Then she went to the loo; sitting on the toilet she looked and saw one long dark hair lying in the bottom of the bathtub. 'Someone has been here, drinking tea,' she thought. 'Whoever it was took a bath.' Walking into the front room, Carrie noticed a note beside the phone, with some coins on it. It read: 'Debbie rang. Here's some money for some calls I made to Oxford.' It was Howard, of course, Carrie recognized the writing. Her heart was beating fast now, she felt violated and at the same time very sorry she'd missed him. In a kind of emotional reflex, she took her notebook, and sat down to write. Opening the page, she saw his writing again. She felt her neck blush, reddening, as her eyes flew across the words, taking it in.

SONG
I I I I I me me me me meee
I I I I I me me me me meee
Me mine me mine me mine me mine I I I self
Me I me mine me I me mine my my my my self
meself myself meself myself mine I mine I mee
I I I I I mee me mee me mee

BY MYSELF

Terrified, she immediately leafed through the whole note-book, scanning quickly, panicking, to see what Howard might have read. Then the anger rose thick in her throat, and she looked up. There was a picture on her wall, a small reproduction of a painting called *Crime Passionel*; it showed a woman shooting a man. Yellow fire burst out of the gun, red blood dripped from his brow onto the floor. For one moment, Carrie wanted a gun. She felt like killing somebody.

She read: *The theme of honour through ruin is fundamental to North-West American potlatch.* Honour through ruin, it could be emblazoned on her shield: an empty cornucopia, perhaps, dripping blood? Melodrama, again, always the resort to melo-drama — if you exaggerate, theatricalize, you can see the absurdity, protect yourself. Carrie was amused to think of her path through life as one great potlatch, or one potlatch after another. Honour through ruin. She read about the Kwakiutl, working through the long winter, how they would carve boxes and canoes, and pile up Hudson's Bay Company blankets, five pairs to a box, and save up the oolachan fish grease, all their luxuries, and then on very specific special occasions, the head of a family or a kinship group would hold a potlatch, and invite everyone, and give it all away.

The more you could give away, the more powerful you were.

The Kwakiutl were obsessed with status: every person of rank had three or four names, linking them to various kinship groups and secret societies, within which they took up carefully differentiated positions in relation to those above and below them in rank. The system was so elaborate that no one was quite equal to anyone else. Each time such a position was taken up, a name and its associated privileges was claimed, a potlatch had to be given. The guests in effect approved the claim, by witnessing the ritual dances, taking part in the feasts, and by accepting gifts suitable to each guest's rank and position. The tally-keeper memorized precisely who received what, as if to preclude later controversy.

Apart from claiming your name and position, the other occasion on which a potlatch could occur, the other great function of potlatches, was in order to wipe out shame.

Of course the Anglos couldn't make it out at all, and predictably, the government tried their best to suppress the practice of potlatch. Meanwhile the Indians continued to hold secret, underground potlatches. At one point in the 1920s, it was planned that the ceremonial dances would take place before a public audience in the local community centre, like the YMCA, under the guise of a demonstration or exhibition of folk-dancing, and then later in the evening, under cover of darkness, the host and his tally-keeper (who these days was allowed to write everything down instead of memorizing it) would go from house to house, ringing the doorbells, and handing out appropriate gifts in the form of cash. Such were the lengths the Kwakiutl were willing to go in order to perpetuate the celebration of potlatch.

The other great ritual that the Europeans objected to was the Hamatsa dances, the Hamatsa being the highest and most prestigious of the ceremonial secret societies. The dancers personified a terrible bird-monster who fed on human flesh, and the most thrilling part of the dance was when the Hamatsa, in a state of ecstasy, took great bites out of various members of the audience. European observers were horrified by this bloody spectacle, especially when the dancer would then spit out a great chunk of raw flesh, to the delight of the audience. It transpired later that this apparent cannibalism was a very secret, carefully planned special effect, involving planted stooges (who were rewarded for being cut or bit), as well as effigies, dead animals, sleight of hand, bladders of blood, etc. This sophisticated combination of elaborate stage manipulation, sado-masochistic display, and extreme frenzy was incomprehensible to the empire builders, who banned the Hamatsa dances also.

The Kwakiutl were always enthusiastic traders with the Europeans, exchanging furs for Hudson's Bay Company blankets (mass-produced in the mills of Yorkshire), and copper sheeting, to make coppers, and steel tools with which they developed the already very advanced art of carving masks and boxes and canoes and totem poles. Eventually, at the potlatch, they were giving away sewing machines, and willow-pattern china, and crates of oranges, bought with their earnings in the fish-canneries and the brothels.

The smallpox epidemics of the 1860s wiped out one-third of the Indian population of British Columbia. One outcome of this decimation was a dramatic breakdown in the elaborate system of rank and status, simply because there weren't enough people left to fill all the positions. Rampant and wildcat potlatches followed, in which more and more ostentatious displays of reckless expenditure took place. A late version of potlatch pushed this excessive expenditure further, towards sheer waste, where instead of giving all this stuff away, it would simply be destroyed. They would build a shelter like a barn, and heap up all the blankets and boxes and canoes and fish grease and sewing machines, and then set fire to it.

When William Duncan set up Metlakatla, these things were forbidden: 'The Demoniacal Rites called Medicine Work; Conjuring and all the heathen practices over the sick; Use of intoxicating liquor; Gambling; Painting Faces; Giving away property for display; tearing up property in anger or to wipe out disgrace.'

Carrie stopped. In this great battle, Jo's name could be something like Throwaway Friendship, but Carrie's was better, tougher — she would be called Destroyer of Love. Waste, sacrifice, rivalry, gift: in the logic of potlatch, the most powerful name belongs to the one who remains empty-handed.

I would like to acknowledge my use of the following books in writing this piece: Captured Heritage, *by Douglas Cole (1985)*; Indian Art of the North West Coast, *by Bill Holm and Bill Reid (1975)*; William Duncan of Metlakatla, *by Jean Usher (1974).*

Also published by Serpent's Tail

The Seven Deadly Sins
Alison Fell (ed.)

'Seven fine writers, seven vices probed to the quick. Splendid.' ANGELA CARTER

'These seven writers represent . . . a newer and more knowing feminist strategy . . . Mischievous and exhilarating.' LORNA SAGE, *The Observer*

'Rich in experiment and imagination, a sign of just how far contemporary women's writing might go.' HELEN BIRCH, *City Limits*

'All of these stories cut deeply and with a sharp edge into the main business of life — death, God and the devil.' RICHARD NORTH, *New Musical Express*

'A rich but random survey of recent women's writing.' JONATHAN COE, *The Guardian*

'An exciting, imaginative mix of stories.' ELIZABETH BURNS, *The List*

'Witty, modern, female.' KATHLEEN JAMIE, *Scotland on Sunday*

'Extremely entertaining.' EMMA DALLY, *Cosmopolitan*

240 pages £7.00 (paper)

From Sleep Unbound
Andrée Chedid

'Andrée Chedid tells this story as though she were a jeweller assembling a bomb; her precision and grace (and those of her translator) are remorseless.'

HARRIETT GILBERT

'*From Sleep Unbound* captures not one woman's world, but that of *all* women, whether . . . cloistered and closeted in a society bound by retrograde customs or in a modern metropolis, liberated for all intents and purposes, but imprisoned within their own psychological cells.'   BETTINA KNAPP

'A brilliant, touching book.'

VICTORIA BRITTAIN, *The Guardian*

'A passionate study of life imprisonment.'

JENNY DISKI, *New Statesman*

'Chedid's spare but beautiful prose makes of this uneventful life a moving parable of oppression and the human spirit's capacity to fight it.'   *7 Days*

'A deep, poetic meticulous exploration of the mind and history of . . . a woman who liberates herself by killing the husband who has tyrannized her.' *TLS*

'Chedid's beautiful tale is a timely reminder that the freedoms Western women take for granted concern them alone.'   *City Limits*

160 pages £4.95 (paper)

The Piano Teacher
Elfriede Jelinek

'A bravura performance.'

SHENA MACKAY, *Sunday Times*

'Good books, like haircuts, should fill you with awe, change your life, or make you long for another. Elfriede Jelinek's *The Piano Teacher* manages to fulfil at least two of these demands in a reckless recital that is difficult to read and difficult to stop reading. The racy, relentless, consuming style is a metaphor for passion: impossible to ignore.'

CAROLE MORIN, *New Statesman & Society*

'Something of a land-mine . . . a brilliant, deadly book.'   ELIZABETH J. YOUNG, *City Limits*

'Some may see, in the pain of this novel, its panic and its deep despair, a model of current writing. For others, *The Piano Teacher* will remain a perverse horror story of a mother's love taken to its logical, deadly extreme.'

ANGELA McROBBIE, *The Independent*

288 pages £7.95 (paper)

Dreaming of Dead People
Rosalind Belben

'Rosalind Belben's eye for the movement and texture of the natural world is extraordinarily acute and she has a poet's ear for language. Her book, although apparently a cry of loneliness and deprivation, is also a confession of fulfilment, of endless curiosity for, and love of, life.' SELINA HASTINGS, *The Daily Telegraph*

'Her heroine is a solitary woman who is suffering as she reconciles herself to loneliness and sterility. She tells of her past and recalls, often, the countryside, where being alone is not painful and, if there is no meaning to life, the call to the senses is immediate. The book is beautifully written ... it will not, repeat *not*, make an acceptable Christmas gift for a person living alone.' HILARY BAILEY, *The Guardian*

'So extraordinarily good that one wants more, recognizing a writer who can conjure an inner life spirit, can envisage, in unconnected episodes, a complete world: one unified not by external circumstances but by patterns of the writer's mind.'
ISABEL QUIGLY, *The Financial Times*

'Some of the most memorable prose in contemporary fiction.' LINDA BRANDON, *The Independent*

'Rosalind Belben's gift or burden is to press on to the painful edge of what is possible. It is an achievement to celebrate.' MAGGIE GEE, *The Observer*

176 pages £6.95 (paper)

Is Beauty Good
Rosalind Belben

'A startling record of life preserved in the face of increasing desolation . . . Rosalind Belben's gift or burden is to press on to the painful edge of what is possible. It is an achievement to celebrate.'
MAGGIE GEE, *The Observer*

'In her work Belben gives us glimpses of such beauty that one can only choose, like her, to celebrate life.'
LINDA BRANDON, *The Independent*

'Spare, lucid prose, reminiscent of Woolf's *The Waves.*'   *The Guardian*

'Belben has an ability to tap deeply into the process of thought itself with all its fragmentation, puns, jokes, obscenities and moments of transfiguration . . . In this case beauty is certainly good.'
ELIZABETH J. YOUNG, *City Limits*

128 pages £6.95 (paper)

Without Falling
Leslie Dick

'A debut of great conviction and profound originality.'
New Musical Express

'A boldly overambitious novel . . . promising stuff.'
Blitz

'Thankfully a million miles from the rosily worthy world of seventies feminist fiction.'
Women's Review

'It is rare these days to find a novel which is so fresh, harsh, exciting and funny.'   *New Statesman*

'In a literary culture dominated by gentility and middlebrowism, *Without Falling* is itself something of a bomb.'   *London Review of Books*

160 pages £5.95 (paper)

Also published by Serpent's Tail

The Passport
Herta Müller

'A haunting and original novel that's both satire and elegy.'   MICHÈLE ROBERTS, *City Limits*

'Herta Müller's language is the purest poetry. Every sentence has the rhythm of poetry, indeed is a poem or a painting.'   *Nürnberger Nachrichten*

'Each short chapter has a title like a poem, and that is precisely what they are, cantos, prose poems, rhythmic texts.'   *Neue Zürcher Zeitung*

96 pages £4.95 (paper)